Sun
8054
Ellicott
(301) 465-0246

What follows is a true story related by an immortal named Addison who has communicated with the mortal plane through the mediumship of Margaret and Maurine Moon.

The "world beyond," according to Addison, is one in which mortals must work out their spiritual progress in terms of what they have brought with them from the other world, realizing that what they learn and do are integral parts of some larger order directed at the raising of consciousness, level by level, to the direct apprehension of Truth.

"Out of the oneness, his form began to emerge, in tactile sense first, for she could feel his body, tall against her own. Then she could see the folds of his shirt that lay on arms that were holding her, hard. And now she knew she could hear him, as well, when she heard, where his face pressed, that tiny sound, that sound like the tearing of silk...."

Eve has a spirit-lover. They have loved in successive incarnations, but only a dim memory remains—enough to make her restlessly yearn for her spiritual home. Their difficult relationship is resolved by the birth of a child whose promise is no less than the spiritual progress of mankind.

SUN SIGN SHOPPE
5710 NEWBURY STREET
MOUNT WASHINGTON VILLAGE
BALTIMORE, MD. 21209
(301) 466-1700

The Jupiter Experiment

A Love Story of This World and the Next

by Margaret and Maurine Moon
from Addison

1976
Llewellyn Publications
Saint Paul, Minnesota, 55165, U. S. A.

© 1976 by Wilcoxon, Inc.

All rights reserved
No part of this book, either in part or in whole,
may be reproduced, transmitted or utilized in
any form or by any means, electronic or
mechanical, including photocopying, recording,
or by any information storage and retrieval
system, without permission in writing from the
publisher, except for brief quotations embodied
in critical articles or reviews.

First Edition 1976

cover designed by Lynette Arndt Schmidt
painting of Addison by Margaret Moon

Llewellyn Publications
Post Office Box 3383
Saint Paul, Minnesota 55165

International Standard Book Number: 0-87542-498-8
Library of Congress Catalog Card Number: 76-3897
Printed in the United States of America

Part One	1
Part Two	21
Part Three	91
Part Four	149
Afterword	203

I want to be with you—
 that is the sum of it.
Oh, take me while the body sleeps
 and hold me fitted to you as I used to be.
The song that drew me once has faded, died away.
The night is cold
 and I am lonely here.

PART ONE

In a century almost beyond memory, on an island which now lies beneath the sea, the story begins ... that is, if indeed there was a beginning any more than there will be an end.

Kapi waited outside the longhut. The Council had been meeting within its fronded walls throughout the night, and Kapi had crouched there, half drowsing through the starry hours. The moon had kept her face hidden, refusing to lend her tender influence to the debate which was in progress, and therefore the Sun would rise alone, in all his fierceness. With dread, Kapi considered the inevitable sternness with which the lone and all-powerful Sun would receive the decision of his father, the king, whatever it should be.

His thin body ached with the tension of his long vigil, and sleep came near to claiming him just as the black dark began to retreat before the Sun, still unseen but inexorably on his way, bringing no mercy in his terrible fire.

Kapi was aroused by the chant sounding from within the longhut. The Council was ending, and the elders would emerge, preceding the king's person, and following behind, in the ancient way, for the king's protection. Without difficulty, Kapi concealed his slight child's body behind the entrance gods. Yes, there in the center of the elders walked his father. He still bore upon his head and shoulders the heavy royal headdress, but now over his belt they had placed the girdle of gold, and on his shoulders lay the great King's Prayer Cape of golden feathers, falling to his feet.

Ah, then ... there had been no decision. His father must go to seek the Sun, and there await a sign.

Passing through the stone cavern leading out of the city, the king turned his face back for a moment to the stone god behind which his young son was hiding himself, his form invisible, surely, in the predawn light.

Kapi, knowing that his father, as Son of the Sun, could see and sense beyond the power of common man, returned the king's unspoken message, using the same divine power which was his power as well by right of succession.

"Yes," was his silent answer. "I will go to her."

When he entered the hut it was still dark, and the family lay quietly on their mats, but Kapi knew they were not sleeping. His mother lay near the doorway, and hearing her irregular breathing, Kapi moved close, to stand beside her so that if she wished to speak to him she need only whisper. She was silent, but he felt her hand for a moment upon his bare foot, holding tightly.

At the end of the room his sister sat upon her mat, and in the faint light he could see her slender arms hugging her knees as though she were in pain.

"Kapi . . ." she began, but could not speak any more.

"Yes," whispered Kapi, "it is over. Father has gone to the cliff."

She began to tremble slightly.

"Lie on my mat, little one," she said at last. "Warm me."

Kapi lay cradled against her, and his thoughts turned back, back, to memories of her, of Pilua, herself a child, holding him in her arms in the water, the cool water of the pool, it must have been. She was laughing, saying, "Come, Kapi, splash!"

He closed his eyes against the pictures, against their childhood. It was over, forever over for them.

Beneath his cheek he could feel the fluttering of her heart. In the open doorway, now, strong rays of red morning light appeared. The Sun. He had come.

Pilua, waiting for Manala, sat well out of the reach of the ocean spray. The sand was wet from the morning tide and seemed to her to breathe a chill fog which penetrated her shaking body. She drew her heavy hair about her for protection—against the wind, against the unknown, against the Sun himself.

And now she saw Kapi limping down the shore in her direction, his lame foot swollen and heavy, so heavy for the thin legs; and rising from the spot where she had crouched, hiding beneath the dark cape of her hair, she ran to meet him and so spare his foot.

She caught him to her as they met, and with surprise she realized that Kapi was growing taller rapidly. His head reached almost to her breast. How fast the time had gone, the days, the nights.

"Manala is not coming," Kapi said, breathlessly, for he was very weary. "He sent me to tell you that he too has gone to the Holy Cliff."

Pilua sat down quickly, unable to stand. "He will be gone all day, and through the night too, if he has gone to the cliff," she told Kapi. "I cannot bear it. I need him."

"But he seeks the Sun, to intercede for you," protested Kapi. "Maybe the Sun will relent, for Manala is dear to him."

"No," replied Pilua. "Manala is angry at the Sun. The Sun will punish him."

Slowly, her arm about Kapi's thin shoulders, Pilua began to walk up the shore toward the city.

As he passed from the shade of the grove into the brightness of the stony gorge, Manala set his widespreading fern headpiece firmly upon his brow. It would be better if the Sun did not become aware of his approach as yet. The rocky hillside rose steeply before him, stretching some distance ahead, and beyond rose the mighty promontory. Against the solid wall of red rock the sea gods had hurled their force both day and night since before memory began, but the Sun had lent his protection to his holy place and the cliff remained towering, still sharp with crags and ledges. It would take some hours yet for the rest of the journey. Manala, hidden under his headpiece, would make his way unseen to the summit and pass the night there, so that in the morning he would catch the Sun unaware and well before he had gathered to himself his fiercest midday strength.

Manala's anger was abating now, and in its place arose bewilderment, a sense of puzzlement. All of his life he had, like his ancestors before him, revered the Sun, obeyed, loved, and feared him. The Sun was the Supreme God, beside whom the lesser gods of the earth were as nothing; giver of all life, the only source, without whom life, once given, could not be sustained; unfailing supply of comfort, light, warmth and beauty; a magnificent god, well worthy of appreciation, deserving of propitiation. Manala still felt from the depths of his being that this was true. Why, then, his boyhood past and manhood upon him, was he now disobedient? And being disobedient, why was he not contrite?

Manala lifted his face to gaze upward to the summit. Out of his sight, among the crags and boulders somewhere far ahead, the king, he knew, was climbing, making his solitary journey, his quest for guidance. It would be unlawful for any man to speak to the king until his prayer had ended, even if Manala were able to overtake him. And of what avail would words be now? The king would not petition the Sun on behalf of his own family, Manala knew, for this too would be unlawful. Son of the Sun, the human embodiment of the Sun himself, the king's primary function was to preserve the divine spark, the royal bloodline. Should the human part of him falter, the Council would enforce the hallowed marriage laws. This was good and right. The city must be assured of a divine representative.

Young Kapi, as the divine successor, was bound by law to take his sister as his royal mate, in order that the bloodline remain pure, that the heir be truly a Son of the Sun. Pilua, the only sister, must inevitably, then, become the royal mother of Kapi's child. The king in his compassion readily understood the tragedy thus imposed upon his family. Kapi was more son than brother to Pilua, who was united in love with Manala. Boldly, the king had proposed an amendment to the law on the grounds that by the time Kapi reached the age for begetting an heir, Pilua would have passed by her maidenhood, and that a substitute mother queen would insure the many sons for which the Council had hoped. The meeting of the Council had continued throughout the night. Did the length of the meeting mean that the Council was at least considering the king's proposal?

Manala, beginning to feel the heat of late morning, selected an outcropping of stone under which to secrete himself from the scrutiny of the Sun—the Sun who would be fully alert as he neared the zenith of his power—and removing his headpiece, sat for a moment's rest.

His thoughts turned to Pilua, as she waited—waited to know her fate, waited for his return. Was he really powerless to protect their love? A bit wildly he thought, I will take her away, away from this place, away from the Council, away from the akahune and his priestly incantations. If there were to be a price to be paid for such insurrection, then they would pay it, together. A boat. No, a sea-worthy craft, one of the pirakuu, he would take it, and take Pilua in it, to the reef. From there he could find the course to the outer islands ... if the sea gods would let them pass. Yes, perhaps they could pass safely, for they would be fleeing from the Sun, and frequently the sea gods warred against the Sun, for they hated his fire. Perhaps they would even give help....

Resolutely Manala rose. Setting his headpiece firmly in place, he began to climb the face of the cliff.

During the afternoon the wind began to rise. Manala had difficulty in keeping his headpiece from being taken by the wind, leaving him exposed to the eye of the Sun. Far below, the sea fought the wind, its ancient enemy, at first sullenly but later with growing defiance.

When he reached the summit, the full force of the gale struck him and Manala covered his stinging eyes. When he could, he looked about the flat surface of the crest, searching for the king, who might still be at prayer upon the peak, but Manala could see no sign save for a golden feather escaped from the king's prayer cape.

Late daylight still remained, and Manala ran to the edge of the summit, sweeping his eyes down upon the path that the king would take on his all-night journey back to the city. At last he could make out the figure of the king halfway down the cliffside, saw him climbing slowly and carefully down, the huge prayer cape over one arm. As Manala watched, incredulous, the king's body swayed, and then with a dreamlike slowness the fall began: over, striking the crags, over, and striking again.... Manala began to run, and desperately, then, to descend the cliff. The wind tore at him, but he spat in its face. His fern headpiece was gone now, but Manala fought his way from ledge to ledge uncaring....

Borne in upon the great wind, the tropic rain suddenly descended from the darkened sky, hurling itself in rage against the rugged face of the cliff. As Manala reached the great boulder near whose base the king lay, he could see the rain already streaming across the closed face, slashing at the bare ground. Manala knelt, pressing his face against the broad chest of the king. So acute did anguish render his senses that he could hear, despite the roar of wind and rain, the faint beating of the heart.

Unable to bear the sight of the unprotected face, Manala ran back up the slope, and jerked the feather prayer cape from the jutting rock where it had fallen, forgetting in his urgency that it was forbidden for any common man to touch it. Racing back to the king's side, Manala flung the cape across the boulder, draping the wide folds to form a shelter, securing it with stones. Blood gushed from the wounded body. Both legs were strangely angled. The king lay as one dead.

Stripping off his loincloth, Manala tried to staunch the blood, but the red flow rose, rose, and continued to rise. It was to no avail. He must go for help. And also, he must bring the akahune to the king, and at once.

He began to run, naked, through the menacing rain, looking back only once, and then quickly, at the golden mound where lay the Son.

It did not matter now that his own holy confrontation had never come to pass. The king had petitioned the Sun, and the Sun had answered.

The rain beat steadily upon the city as word spread, and in the open doorways torches flickered, struggling against the storm. The rescue procession set out long before dawn, a very short time after Manala had brought his news. For him, there was time only to clothe himself and to take from a gourd the few mouthfuls he was able to swallow before setting out again to guide the way to the spot where the king lay.

But in the city the turmoil continued. Did the king still live? Had the Sun struck a mortal blow? Was there yet hope for them? If the king lay dead upon the slope, then there remained to his people but one link with the Sun himself, the male child, Kapi. Kapi, where was he at this moment? Who had seen him and remembered? Through the storm the people gathered before the king's hut.

When the queen appeared before them, they fell silent, seeing her face. No words need be spoken. The prince was gone.

The people had pressed closely about Manala when he had come bearing the dreadful news. Kapi had seen him searching the dark rain, unable to find Pilua where she stood, as still as one turned to stone, unable to speak or to make her way through the throng to Manala. Tearing his eyes from Manala's distorted face, Kapi had stared, fascinated, at his sister. Even in the uncertain torchlight flaring through the rain, he had seen her great dark eyes fixed upon Manala, and the thing he saw written upon her once beautiful, young face had filled Kapi with such terror as he had known but once before, when the great squid had appeared among the children swimming in the surf.

When at last Pilua could move, she did not press through the crowd to fling herself upon Manala, weeping, as he had seen her do the day before, yes, and the day before that, also. To Kapi's astonishment, he saw Pilua stepping backward, away, silently fading out of sight in the darkness. Kapi, following, could not at first see where she had gone. But then, ahead, he could hear her running feet splashing through the waters which streamed through the grove.

Wildly he scrambled, slipping in the muddy water, dragging his heavy foot as fast as he could pull and lift, pull and lift, but Pilua was fleeing with such frantic speed that Kapi knew he could not keep up with her, would perhaps lose her trail. Nevertheless, the little boy pressed on.

At first Kapi judged that Pilua, after passing through the grove, must be making toward the place where Manala had said they would begin the climb up the side of the promontory to where the king had fallen. But now he could hear her steps turning toward the sea.

For a time Kapi lost the sounds of her flight, but he continued through the blackness, groping in the direction of the shore. The sea gods were crying out loudly, hurling back the attack of the winds, and such was the clamor of battle that Kapi despaired of hearing Pilua's steps.

He paused, gasping for breath, trying to feel an inner voice moving silently behind his closed eyes. He knew the king had access to this soundless voice, and now in his extremity Kapi waited. But no impression brushed feather-like within, as he had heard it described by the akahune. Well then, and would no god guide him?

Far ahead he heard above the turbulence a faint cry, as of pain or fear. Perhaps Pilua had stumbled, fallen, was hurt.... He urged his chilling body on, faster than he had been able to progress before, keeping in his pounding heart the sound of her cry and making blindly toward the remembered sound.

The darkness was now less thickly clotted before him. Faintly, he could see the outline of the promontory, oil-black against a still-black sky. The Sun was on his way, covering his angry face with the headdress of the storm.

Suddenly Kapi felt the wet stone slab slanting under his feet, and a breaker struck him down, pitching him into shallow water. He had reached the sea and as he flailed with his thin arms, desperately clawing for something, some stone or twisted root, to cling to, Kapi felt the feather brushing behind his eyes—at first hardly discernible to his distracted mind, and then, again, unmistakably the harsh, strong feather of a sea bird. The sea gods, then, had come to him.

It was then that Kapi knew, at once, where he was. He had played here with Pilua long ago, many times, in the small cove which circled its way gently into the base of the cliff at the place where the monstrous stone approached the sea. Near this place had stood the ancient city, in that forgotten time before the grove existed, before the reefs and beaches had formed. Close against the cliff itself one of the gods remained, an enormous figure, still seated on the solid rock of the promontory, partly submerged now in the waves and the waters of the sea. Kapi had wanted to climb upon it, playing, but Pilua had said perhaps the god still watched there, though the city had perished, before memory; he must be treated with respect, she had said. Yes, this was the massive, time-pitted arm of the god to which Kapi now clung as the breakers' crushing force struck him again and again.

Once more the sea bird's feather stroked swiftly behind Kapi's straining eyes. Though the darkness pressed upon him, he could see quite clearly in memory the remnants of the stairway curving upward along the sheer face of the cliff, the stones, carved out so long ago by the ancient ones, leading up to the Holy Place, the flattened ceremonial crest. With certainty now, Kapi knew that Pilua was making her way toward that crest, and that she had chosen to come this way, through the old city, because it was a shorter distance from home than the path up the slopes where Manala would be leading the akahune and the rescue party. Pilua meant to reach the crest with all possible speed, while yet there remained hope in her that the king still lived.

And Pilua would attempt to intercede for the king, with an angry god who turned away his face!

In the horror of his comprehension, Kapi could recall of the ancient stairway only that as the stone god sat facing the sea, the cliff lay close to the back of the great silent figure. Groping blindly, reaching with his good leg, he found at last the jutting wall of rock and flung himself upon it. Scrambling on hands and knees like a small wounded crab, he pulled himself from the surf and when his hands discovered the first step, unmistakable to his tracing fingers because of its rounded edge, he began to creep slowly upward.

As he climbed, leaving the sea below, Kapi thought at times that he could hear Pilua climbing slowly far ahead, but he could not be certain. His great heavy foot was bruised and bleeding and his progress was so slow that he wished he could send his spirit out of him, as the akahune often did—yes, dispatch his spirit, instructing it to leave the small and crippled body and go, go upward seeking Pilua, overtaking her, overpowering her, turning her feet about and bringing her back, away from the Holy Crest which loomed so near. . . .

The rain continued but had ceased its slashing, so

that it fell in heavy streams before the slackening wind. Kapi could see the shape and contours of the crest in the paling sky. Gratefully he realized that the Sun was drawing close and that his approach had subdued the violence of the storm.

Forced by fatigue to pause for a moment in his climb, Kapi could now view the ceremonial crest, its strange sheared-off surface exposed against the universe, suspended in space as if floating there. Searching with both mind and soul, through aching eyes he made out the blurred but undeniable form of Pilua, on her knees, supporting her body with her arms, her hair a dark shadow, snakelike in the wet, falling past her face and forming an indistinct mound upon the ground.

Kapi, transfixed, watched from his position on the stairs, in a state which was ever after to be his lot—near enough to see, but not close enough to cry out, to make her aware of his nearness. Immobilized by his condition, he watched with haunted eyes, and within him there was no surprise as Pilua arose and began to dance.

She moved falteringly with the strength remaining to her, in the dance which Kapi knew was the only dance left to her—the ultimate propitiatory dance, the Death Dance for the forgiveness of the Sun, who had not yet arrived, and who, when he did appear, would still draw his headdress across his face.

Fleetingly Kapi thought of Manala. By now Manala would have reached the king, might even be bearing him back to his people. Was the king still alive? Could the sacrificial dance of Pilua persuade the Sun to spare the Son to his city, seeing that Kapi was too young to represent the god? Ah, and if the Sun had taken him, then even more surely must Pilua dance.

It was too late for Manala, and too late also for Kapi, he knew. It was now between Pilua and the god himself. She could be trusted to fulfill the law. And that was right. But he had never seen the sacrifice performed in this terrifying way. To dance alone, in the near dark, her wet hair coiling cold about her body ... dancing painfully, without grace ... fully, entirely conscious.... Yearningly, he wished for her the sacred tea, to bring her visions ... the flowers for her hair ... the entire city in attendance, and the other maidens dancing with her ... the Council present in ceremonial robes, and the akahune to give the incantation which would cancel out her fear....

Kapi clung to the stone steps with his entire body. He could see her distinctly now. He could see the desperate straining of her weakened body to execute the ancient dance in its perfection, so that it should be pleasing to the approaching Sun.

When he saw her stumble, panic overcame him and he screamed, "Leap! Leap now, Pilua!" not caring that she could not hear, for she must thrust her body out as she leaped, soaring away from the cliff, in order to fall into the gorge far below. Kapi had thought that when the dance was finished he could not watch, but now he knew he must watch, long enough to see whether in her fall she could clear the jutting shapes of rock below the crest, falling free, into the Land of the Sun.

He could tell that Pilua knew her strength was ebbing, because she omitted the ritual of the thighs and too slowly, pathetically, she began the final ritual of the breast, but she could not sustain the motion. Now ... yes, now ...

He did not really believe it when he saw the fall

begin. To him she seemed to be a phantom, dropping strangely, too close, too close to the cliff. In her flight, the phantom fell past him where he grappled with the stone to keep from falling himself. Droplets of water from her hair fell upon his face as she glided down past him, and he followed the unreal figure with incredulous eyes. She was no longer Pilua now, but a goddess, flying beyond his reach....

But when he saw the ledge where she had fallen, far, far above the gorge, too near, much too near the crest, he knew she was still Pilua, for as he looked down the cliffside upon her where she lay, he saw that she was trying to lift her arms but could not. She had failed. She should be in the Land of the Sun by now, her body forgotten at the bottom of the gorge, her aka body perfect, free.... But she had failed, and lay still living upon the ledge below. Sobbing, Kapi began to drag and lift, drag and lift, crawling when need be, inching his way downward toward the ledge. He could not remember when the rain had stopped, because all he could remember now were the drops of water flung upon him from her hair.

She lay upon the cruel crag, her face turned to the sky, her legs hanging over the sharp edge. Kapi could see no blood upon her, but the stones were splattered red, and thin dark trickles ran across the ledge and dripped rapidly over, and down into the distant gorge.

He wanted to shout her name, feeling that if only he could rouse her she would open her eyes, would see that she was not alone, but no sound came from his burning throat. Irrationally, he could not bear the sight of the vicious rock cutting into her smooth thighs and he began to tug at her body, pushing, sliding, once nearly falling from the crag, until he had managed to place her wholly upon the ledge in what seemed to his distraught mind to be a position of repose. Only then did he begin to quiver, a terrible quivering that shook his body, and weakness forced him to his knees. As he continued to kneel, watching the quiet face, Pilua opened her eyes as if returning his gaze, but he could not tell whether she could see. When at last the eyelids closed, she opened them no more.

The first rays of the victorious Sun found them easily enough, and when Kapi lifted his face to the god in greeting, he knew that Pilua had departed, claimed by the Sun, her aka body whole, lithe and once more beautiful. The Sun would welcome her. The city was safe.

But the tremor in his thin body was still uncontrollable. It was difficult for him to cling to the ledge. Slowly he lowered himself upon the stone, lying close through the long hours, curled against her body as in his early years. It was so that Manala found them as he came searching.

Manala was moving very slowly, carrying Pilua's body from ledge to ledge, but even so it was impossible for Kapi to keep up. When Manala reached the stairway he looked back, and seeing Kapi's struggle he paused, waiting so that they could descend the steps together. Manala had not spoken, even when Kapi had tried to find voice to tell him what had happened, and Kapi had fallen silent before the look upon Manala.

When they reached the bottom of the stairs, the cove lay shallow and tranquil in the early sunshine. Incredibly, the hideous features of the stone god remained unmoved by the sorrows of the night. He sat smugly as he had always sat, endlessly contemplating his enemy, the sea. In his half-demented mind Kapi wondered whether, as Pilua had suspected, the ancient god still had power. And if the stone god yet lived, was he uncaring or was he unknowing of what had passed this night?

Manala laid Pilua on the flat stone slab which slanted into the cove, and taking his headband from his brow, he wet it in the clear water and began to bathe the darkening blood from her body. Suddenly he dropped the band and sweeping Pilua up into his arms against his breast—it, too, red with her blood—he whirled, turning his back against the brightening Sun, and faced the sea. Kapi knew, quite clearly, that Manala meant to carry her into the water, to take her out beyond return, to let the sea take them both. But Manala turned about when he heard Kapi's shriek, and at last he placed Pilua back upon the slab. Turning to Kapi, he said, "I cannot leave you, Son of the Sun."

They rested, cleansing themselves in the sea, and speaking little.

Finally Kapi asked, "Why did the Sun take my father and leave me, a crippled child, as king?"

"The Sun did not take the king," answered Manala, "nor did he require the sacrifice of Pilua."

Stunned, Kapi could not speak.

"The law took them," continued Manala, "the ancient law...." He gazed out across the water for a long moment. "The stone god," he said. "It was only the stone god, Kapi."

PART TWO

*Shall we gather at the river
 where bright angel feet have trod,
  with its crystal tide forever
   flowing by the throne of God?*

—old hymn by ROBERT LOWRY

IM (Immortal) level, 1952

Major Max Melchior was late getting to the office. As he walked down the marble corridor he felt the diminishing of the auric field surrounding his body and knew that he must have a moment's privacy sometime during the morning in order to recharge. The night's caseload had been heavier than usual. He would have to turn part of it over to Ida. If she didn't come in this morning, he would flash her.

As he entered his outer office, his aide Fleming looked up from the desk to say warningly, "Max, they sent over a special from Receiving a few minutes ago. I put her in your private office."

"Damn," said Max, flashing for service, "I had a rough night. I wanted coffee before starting work."

"Sorry," Fleming said, handing him a sheaf of papers, "but the patient was unmanageable at Receiving. I had to keep her here."

"Well, get me a clean shirt and when the coffee comes bring it to my dressing room."

Max went into his dressing room, examining the papers as he unbuttoned his uniform. The report on the special: violent transition, instantaneous, auto wreck ... unaccompanied ... estimated age, late teens ... attitude, negative ... other readings, negative ... no restraint applied, special interview requested. Wow, those war casualties last night, and now this!

Removing his shirt, Max caught sight of himself in the broad mirror over the stone basin. What the hell, how had the grey hair happened to show up at his temples? He hadn't mocked it up, not consciously. Must have thought at the sub level that he needed it to maintain an image of authority. Well, didn't look too bad, at that.

The coffee came, and Max poured some into a mug before he realized he could not take time to drink it. He flashed for service and told the waiter. "Take this into my private office. And bring another mug."

"Yes sir, Major," said the waiter. "Could I bring you a cinnamon roll? You seem tired, sir."

"Great," said Max, tying his tie, "and thank you, Cummings. Oh," he added as the boy was leaving, "get service up here to change the champagne. I wanted it in small bottles."

Passing through the outer office, he stopped at Flemings's desk. His eyes were stinging and he felt the fatigue in his arms as he reached for the communicator. Reconsidering, he said to Fleming, "Get Ida up here right away, and then contact the sensitives and see whether they can give me an hour about nine tonight, M-time." He opened the double doors to his office and went in.

The girl stood stiffly in the center of the room, looking at him. She was very small. Her black hair fluffed in disarray around her face. Her eyes were stony.

"Please sit down," he said to the patient.

She did not move.

"Can you tell me your name?"

She did not speak.

"Are you aware of what has happened, sweetie?" he asked, getting up and going toward her.

The waiter came in with the coffee and at a nod from Max handed a steaming cup to the girl. She threw it on the floor. Just like Ida was when she first came over, Max said to himself, only Ida had yelled a lot. The silent ones were harder to deal with. Where was Ida, anyhow?

The doors swept open and the insouciant Ida sauntered into the room. This morning she had fancied holiness and wisdom and was dressed the part, in a monk's robe of thin saffron silk.

"What are you made up for?" Max said, "and where have you been, anyway?"

"Go to hell," answered Ida pleasantly, "Fleming sent for me. What have you botched up now?"

"I've got a list for you, part of mine from last night. And how about taking over this patient here?"

Ida studied the girl, passing her hands along the auric field.

"She's in rebellion," volunteered Max. "That's why the aura is so red."

"No," said Ida, "it's fear."

"Same thing."

"Men!" she said, but fairly mildly. She put both hands on the girl's shoulders. "What's your name?"

"Harriet," said the girl.

"Harriet," Ida asked her, "do you realize that you have a different kind of body now? That's the first thing we want you to accept."

The girl ran, to the right, to the left, frantically, backing up against the wall, almost upsetting the liquor cabinet.

"Watch it, sweetie!" cried Max.

"I shouldn't have touched her," admitted Ida. "I told you, it's fear."

"There's always fear," said Max. "Can't you penetrate it? She isn't hearing us."

"No, I can't penetrate it," retorted Ida. "Don't you see what happens in the aura when I project to her?"

"She's thrown up a shield," said Max, checking the girl's electric field. "Somebody at Receiving must have traumatized her. It's a thick purple."

"I can read," reminded Ida, again touching the girl's aura with her open palms. "Look. She doesn't react well to me. See the color change?"

"Right," Max agreed. "Well, there goes that!"

"Where goes what?"

"I was getting ready to ask you to take her home

with you for a while. I can't put her in an institutional environment while she's in this condition. But she's afraid of you."

"I can't think why," replied Ida slowly. "I think you're reading into it from your own bank. She's not afraid of me."

"Maybe you just rub her the wrong way, then. Anyhow the relationship isn't harmonious. It won't work."

"Well, what, then? Maybe you should take her home. Think maybe she's harmonious with you? Go ahead. She can throw coffee at your place."

"I know who," said Max. "Perfect! I'll flash Scott Allen."

"Oh, stop it!" cried Ida. "He's not doing this work any more, you know that. Besides, just because he was so great with your case you think he can do anything, but this girl—just a kid, really—she needs a woman, seems to me. Let's look in the file . . ."

"I have a hunch," Max said. "Get hold of Scott and tell him I need him."

"Lo, how the mighty have fallen!" observed Ida. "I would have said you didn't need anybody."

"Not during working hours, for God's sake," protested Max. "See if you can get this girl to have some coffee. I seem to shake her up."

"And she's not the only one," muttered Ida, turning again toward the girl. "It's all right, Harriet," she said to her. "You don't have to take any of this coffee. But I'll have some myself."

Ida filled a mug from the carafe and began to sip, not looking at the girl. Harriet, unmoved, stared woodenly at the carpet.

"Sorry, Ida," said Max, "I know I asked your help. But I think I'm right."

"Yeah," said Ida.

The communicator glowed. "That'll be Scott," Max said, picking it up. "I love you," he said to her, before speaking into it.

"Yeah," she said.

In the outer office, Ida sat at Max's desk and began to run through the caseload report that lay in a thick sheaf before her—forty-two names, with voluminous notes regarding each. Max had gone through transition with every one of them, personally. In all the years, Ida had never ceased to feel reverence for his capacity to endure the emotion she knew he experienced with each one. She would interview them now, one by one, hoping that Max would continue to sleep in his desk chair in his private office until time for his meeting with staff.

Picking up the communicator, she flashed her own department. "I'm tied up at Major Melchior's office until the staff meeting," she told her secretary. "You'll have to run things until I get back."

"But you have an appointment with Mr. Higgins at eleven o'clock, Miss Adriano," he answered. "What shall I do with him?"

"Suit yourself; I'm broad-minded. Listen, would you mind getting in touch with my house and telling them Major Melchior is coming for dinner, late dinner? And tell my houseman to get that damn fountain fixed by tonight."

"Which fountain is that?"

"The one in my bedroom that has the green water in

it. Well, I want it blue, the shade I told him. And have my designer come to see me right away and tell him I want him to make something for me to wear tonight—something with fur on it—so tell him he should bring his book along."

Ida picked up the list again. She checked one or two names of patients for whom sedation would soon be wearing off. She must get over there to Receiving right away.

She called to Max's aide, "Fleming, I'm off to Receiving for interviews. Flash me when my designer gets here and I'll come back for awhile. Where's that waiter?"

"He's still in Major Melchior's private office, Miss Adriano."

Kicking her skirts out of her way, Ida stepped into Max's inner office. The waiter, relaxed on the sofa, was sipping champagne from a tumbler. "What the hell do you think you're doing, Cummings?"

"Waiting for Major Melchior to wake up."

"What for? Whatever it is you want, you can ask me."

"No ma'am, Miss Adriano. He told me to pour him a glass of champagne and when he wakes up again, I'll hand it to him. He likes it fresh-poured," he explained, as he refilled his glass.

"Oh," said Ida. "Well, happy days in the heavenly realm."

Happy nights, too, she thought. Max was elusive, but certainly not invincible. Fur and bare skin—what a beautiful contrast—and pale turquoise water, falling. Wet shoulders ... jet hair ... oh yes, Max would forget the caseload. Smiling and swinging her skirts, she left the office.

It was dark at first when Eve entered the room and she did not know he was standing at the entrance to the atrium. How perfect it is, she thought, just so—the singing silence, the perfumed darkness—then he turned and swiftly they flowed together, still silent.

Out of the oneness, his form began to emerge, in tactile sense first, for she could feel his body, tall against her own. Then she could see the folds of his shirt that lay on arms that were holding her, hard. And now she knew she could hear him, as well, when she heard, where his face pressed, that tiny sound, that sound like the tearing of silk.

They moved together to the terrace. The night landscape lay there tranquilly, steeped in silver. Across the gleaming river, the distant mountains rose. Home, she thought, the hills of home ... like the old song ... the other song? ... Shenandoah, I'm bound to leave thee. ...

"This is my home," she said to him.

"No. Not for many years yet."

"Scott, I must come here to stay," she whispered.

"No. You cannot . . . must not," was his answer.

He held her, but did not speak.

I have said it at last, Eve thought. I want to die and be with him always. I have told him.

"Beloved—," he said at last, but nothing more.

It was enough.

Death ...

Awake in the night, Scott spoke the word aloud, rejoicing in it. Never had he been chary of the word; he had always preferred it to the term *transition* used by so many of his friends in Project Jupiter. For him, death had meant release, escape, freedom at last. More than that, it had meant homecoming. After his long and unhappy mortal life had come to an end, he had never once looked back upon it with nostalgia. He had resumed his life in this other world, on this immortal level of consciousness, with a sure, accustomed ease. He had moved about, communicated, clothed himself and set about planning his habitation with the facility that would have been his had he never left this beloved land of reality for the dream of mortal life.

For it was indeed as a dream that his time on the mortal level appeared to him now. He thought of it seldom and then fleetingly, recalled it vaguely and in fragments, and it interested him mildly, if at all. He had been a dreamer, grateful to have awakened at last, and he had not encouraged those here who had known him on that sorry voyage to enlighten him concerning it. That the Beloved had shared it, in part, did not mitigate sufficiently his feelings of vague distress over the entire venture, the wisdom of which he doubted, and of which he wished to hear as little as possible.

He left his bed and walked about in the calm of the night. The luminous world about him rested serenely in a thin, silvered mist. Nightwinds brushing his bare shoulders spoke of peace, peace . . . The music of the night was rapt, hushed, spellbound.

But thinking of his death, of his awakening here, had brought for him that other time, and once again it was the turn of the century, and he was an old man of 84, alone, and stiff with pain, and dying.

He had come into the world of spirit gently, in a twilight sleep. For him it seemed a familiar place, as he came and went, came and went, slowly, from sleep to waking. He recognized the faces of those who moved about his room in silence: old friends, some looking much younger than they had in life; his father, no longer grave; his mother unchanged. But he watched them drowsily, as one would regard old photographs, with affectionate nostalgia, without present reality. There was one presence only which absorbed him, blurring all others. The Beloved.

He lay watching her as she sat beside his couch, waiting. There was no urgency to speak. They had both passed through the ordeal of mortal lifetimes and were safely returned home. There would be time enough for them to talk. There would be eternity.

Ah, but it was not to be. Project Jupiter had intervened, and once again they had been parted, this time not by death but by life. The Beloved had been required to re-enter the M-level, remembering him not at all except in the far deeps of her consciousness, from whence she had cried out to him ceaselessly, until at last he was able to bring her to him for short periods of time.

Could it continue—the sharing of these precious hours together which, for him, had given meaning to his existence and, for her, had hushed the yearning voice? Surely, was it not better so? By preserving their consecrated love, were they not enabled to better serve that highr commitment which superseded all transient attachments? The veil had been kept tightly drawn. Eve's mortal life had unfolded naturally, unaffected by any awareness of him, although he remembered everything of her.

But of late there had been a change. There had been

a quickening of Eve's psychic perception. Would she soon begin to recall their times together? God grant that this should never be! Were she to remember him, they would face a bitter choice....

In the night's deepest hour, reaching out for him, Eve found he was not there. She passed quickly through the shadowed rooms, her negligee trailing on the crimson carpets.

He was in the atrium, his naked body reflected in the still water. I'd like a statue of him in that very spot, that very pose, Eve thought as she watched him standing, weight on one hip, head turned toward the mountain view. Coming to him, she saw his face.

"Scott," she said, "what is it?"

They stood silently, holding, holding, pressed against each other.

"We must reach a decision for one course or the other," he said at last. "We have become a danger to the commitment."

Eve swayed slightly and he steadied her.

"You must not come to me again," he told her gently.

"No," she whispered. "The other choice. I must come to stay."

The children—, she thought.

"They are old enough now," she said aloud.

"Yes."

"Warner will manage just fine."

"Yes, darling. He is a good man."

"If I wait until they are older, it would be harder for them to bear."

"And the child here needs you."

Scott lifted her trembling body and began to walk back into the sheltering house.

"Can you do this thing?" he asked. "We must consider."

There is no escape, Eve thought as he carried her. It is torment either way.

In their bedroom he helped her prepare for return to the physical world. Soon, in the simple blue nightgown, she would awaken there.

"When shall it be?" Her voice was quiet.

"We will talk about it when you come again."

She touched his face with her hand as he cradled her in his arms. "That means you have changed your mind?"

"Of course," he answered, and his cheek was wet. "Forgive me for wanting it, Beloved."

She tried to speak but could not. The darkness began and soon she could no longer feel his arms.

"I love you," she heard him say, but she could no longer see him.

The darkness deepened. She slept. . . .

Off the atrium, a small courtyard opened onto a stone walkway leading to the low glass-walled annex belonging to the house steward, Robert. If he had any name other than Robert, he had never mentioned it and neither Scott nor Eve had felt that it mattered enough to ask. He seemed to have been always a part of their lives, and when he had once said that his Polynesian name made him feel like a houseboy, Scott had laughingly dubbed him Robert, saying that name surely was one of sufficient dignity to dispel any suggestion of servitude.

Despite this precaution, Robert desired no other life

than his close association with the lives of Scott and Eve. He had no friends outside their circle, nor did any pursuit intrigue him other than the management of the home, and he was content to fill his days with countless acts of devotion and concern for them. When they pressed Robert on this fact, urging him to make a life of his own, he replied that in his last mortal life he had been so heavily burdened that now, freed from those insupportable pressures, his only desire was sanctuary, and reunion with Scott and Eve with whom he had had connection on the M-level—an association which they did not recall but which Robert treasured.

Robert's age would have been impossible to estimate from his appearance alone. His apparent youth of face and form contrasted dramatically with the ageless aspect of his demeanor. The perfection of his body was marred only by one defect. One foot was misshapen, causing a marked limp in his gait. Always when Eve protested that the deformity was in his consciousness and that he must release it so that the foot could be perfect, Robert replied that he preferred to retain the lame foot, since he thought of it as proof of his identity.

A patient of Major Melchior's was a houseguest, and now Robert, on his way to her room, stopped first at his own suite. As he opened the tall double doors, deeply carved and darkly gleaming, he surveyed the room with pleasure. The white walls were banked on one side with potted trees and ferns, and here the birdcages of spiraled silver hung in dappled light from the paneless window. On the polished tiles, two large rugs of lime-tinted fur made a background for the long, low, padded platform which was his couch. Its cool white linen cover and many brilliant cushions delighted him. He would have liked to lie upon it for a moment, tuning in his music, but he must see to the girl first.

Changing his coat quickly in the simple bedroom adjacent, he left the suite and proceeded down the hall. At Harriet's door he knocked lightly, knowing she would not recognize a beam if he sent it. She did not respond, so Robert entered quietly. The girl cowered away from him. Taken aback and a little hurt, he paused on his progress toward her, his face puzzled. Harriet observed him cautiously.

"Am I then so repellent? Is it my lame foot?" he asked.

Surprise softened her expression. "Oh, no," she protested, "you're okay." As an after-thought, to make sure he understood that this was a high compliment, she added primly, "Actually, you're really good-looking."

"You do not object to the foot, in that case?"

"Why are you talking in that phony accent?" she asked.

"Doubtless because I have been here a long time, since the era in which people spoke in this fashion."

"Well, I wish you'd stop it. It gives me—nerves. Everything in this weird place gives me—nerves."

Robert saw she was having trouble communicating in words, trying to fit her speech to his. He was silent, looking at her intently.

"Why are you looking at me?" she asked, brushing her hair away from her face with one hand, looking at him with her great grey eyes.

"I am listening to your thoughts," replied Robert matter-of-factly.

Harriet lifted an eyebrow, smiling skeptically, daring him.

34

"You are wondering whether I am Oriental," said Robert, smiling, "and now, whether I might be Negro."

She gave him an abashed smile. "Are you?"

"I am Polynesian."

"Do you think I'm rude?"

He did not reply. Suddenly she released the chairback she had been clinging to and sat down rather shakily. "My name is Harriet; what's yours?"

"Robert."

"That's a funny name for a Polynesian."

"I know. Perhaps some day I will tell you about it."

"How long have you been here?"

"A long time."

"I know, but how long?"

"Probably, to you, about three hundred years."

She started to smile but suddenly began to cry. "Oh, Robert, three hundred years! I'll never be able to stand it!" Both hands were pressed to her face. "I want to go home!" she moaned.

Robert touched her hair lightly and said, "You are home, Harriet."

Harriet continued to weep while Robert comforted her, telling her that she would understand all in time. When she stopped crying he stood up to leave, putting her from him a little way and saying with smiling eyes, "Your host has requested me to tender you an invitation to join us at dinner, if the suggestion meets with your approval."

Her flushed face broke into a merry smile. "Oh, Robert," she laughed, and once more searched for words, "you're— you're— you're cute!"

Back in his suite, Robert stretched himself comfortably on his couch, his head on crossed arms, his face to the ceiling where the mosaics swirled in myriad colors and forms. He, who for hundreds of years had had no need of words, reflected musingly upon the thought-cluster Harriet had given him ...

Cute.

I am cute.

He felt fine.

M (Mortal) level, 1952

Eve threw back the lace-edged sheet and sat up in bed. The sun showed hot against the closed draperies. It must be late morning. Rising, she crossed the room, conscious of fatigue. The air conditioner hummed softly and the house was cool and quiet.

A note from Warner lay on her dressing table. "Evie," it read, "you had a bad night so I didn't wake you. Call me when you get up. I might have some good news."

Another restless night. Another night of never quite remembered dreams. Another night that left her weary, vaguely sad, unaccountably lonely. Why? Why? Why? She did not know.

Stepping out of her blue nightgown, she put on a bathing suit and picked up a towel. Perhaps the pool would ease the weariness.

Where were the children? Going down the stairs she saw them through the wide patio doors. The housekeeper, Marsalina, was with them. Good. She loved and trusted Marsalina. The bright California sun hurt her eyes and she put up an arm to shield them as she crossed the flagstones to the pool. This sun-baked land! she thought, and longed once more for the cool green mountains of Virginia, for the home of her childhood.

The two girls came running toward her, their little gold-brown bodies streaming wet. She choked back a compulsive sob at sight of them. What was the matter with her this morning? She caught them close, their wet suits cold on her skin. She shivered. Precious, so precious. More precious than all else. My baby girls.

"Mrs. Temple, I tried to keep them quiet so you could sleep, but you know how they squeal when they play in the pool."

Marsalina ... Eve thought suddenly ... if anything should happen to me, Marsalina would be like a mother to the children— Abruptly, she cut off the thought.

"I'm going in for a short swim, Marsalina, and then let's have some iced coffee out here by the pool."

Plunging into the water, Eve swam slowly, deeply down. The throbbing silence, how strangely familiar it was, how comforting, another world. I like it here, I want to stay here, I don't want to go back up, I want to stay ... silly, get out of the water; Marsalina is waiting with the coffee. ...

Even the sun-heated flagstones did not warm her as she sat, exhausted and shivering, wrapping her towel about her. Marsalina brought coffee to her and poured some for herself. The simple act of solicitude brought a sudden freshet of tears.

"Mrs. Temple!" gasped Marsalina in alarm, "Are you sick? What shall I do?"

Eve got up and went to the table where Marsalina sat under the umbrella, round-eyed and concerned. Trembling, she grasped the back of a chair with one hand, impatiently brushing the tears from her eyes with the other. "How long is it, Marsalina, that you've been with our family?"

"Why, since Kim was born, Mrs. Temple."

Of course. Eve knew exactly when it had been. It had been during the happy years. Before this ... this ... this what?

Something is wrong with me.

Eve walked quickly into the house. Warner's warm voice on the telephone would make everything all right again. It always did.

"You slept late," he said. "Good. Look, I've a little surprise for you. How would you like to fly to Washington for a few days? I've got a few days' business there, and you could see Mary Kay. Think Marsalina could cope with the kids, alone?"

Relief welled within her. "Oh, Warner," she said. "When?"

"We'll leave this weekend if you can make it that soon."

She could not answer.

"Hey, honey, is something wrong? Sounds as though you're crying."

"It's only—," Eve managed at last. "—only that I need so badly to get away—"

Why?

Because for me the world is cold, and I am lonely here.

IM-level

They sat at evening supper in the atrium. This time, Eve told herself, summoning the whole force of her will, this time I want to remember; I *must* remember; I *shall* remember.

The candlelight was light enough. Scott's face across the table from her gleamed like bronze. In his soft, silken beard were golden glints, and on his lips there was a candle-glow.

My love, she thought.

He poured the ruby wine into the glasses, the tall ones of thin crystal with fragile, twisted stems, the glasses that had been his gift to her, because he thought their delicacy was hers.

My love, she thought.

His voice was low upon the evening air. "Remember, Eve, that neither life nor death can sunder, finally, two who are joined by an Almighty Hand." His dedication was upon his face, and in her glowing eyes he saw her own. He smiled his gentle smile and handed her the wine. She reached to take it, her decision made.

He knew. There was no need for words.

My love, she thought.

M-level

Eve sat at her writing desk, idly toying with the feathered pen, her mind in a state of reverie. Her eyelids slowly closed; she leaned her cheek upon her palm, and, dreamily, with eyes still closed, began to write as words welled up within her mind:

> *The candlelight is light enough. His face*
> *Across the table from me gleams like bronze.*
> *The soft and silken beard is golden-glinted,*
> *And on the lips, whose tenderness I know,*
> *There is a candle-glow.... My love.*
>
> *He pours the ruby wine in cherished glasses,*
> *Tall ones of thin crystal, with fragile, spiraled stems,*
> *Glasses that had been his gift to me*
> *Because, he said, their delicacy was mine.... My love.*
>
> *So long ago, so far away in time,*
> *So many anguished lives ago it was*
> *Since we were forced apart. And now I know*
> *That where he is, in life or death, I, too, must be.*
>
> *My choice is made.*
> *And now his face is suddenly so beautiful....*
> *He knows. There is no need for words.... My love.*

Eve read it over, puzzled. What on earth? It didn't make sense. What a romantic fantasy her subconscious mind had come up with! Perhaps something she had read in a book? ... seen in a movie? ... A faint memory stirred....

She hid the poem in her desk drawer along with other poems she had written through the years.

IM-level

"Not bad," said Max, checking the report on it. "Altered a bit here and there, of course, but close enough."

M-level

The telegram arrived just as Mary Kay returned from shopping. Setting down her bundles on the hall table, she tore it open, easing out of her shoes as she stood reading it. Terrific! Eve would be arriving next week! Could it really be happening? The years had gone by so fast since they had been together. How many times they had tried to plan visits! Something had always come up. One or the other of them was pregnant, or building a house or an addition, or putting in a pool, or taking a course at summer school, or helping someone through a hysterectomy—and lately, for both, there had been deep involvement in what Ken called their "do-gooder" activities. Always, a future time seemed promising, but never was. And now, suddenly and without any planning, she was coming!

Too bad Ken was gone. The tests at the field station in Idaho would take him another two weeks. And Warner would be staying downtown most of the time at the hotel where his meetings were being held. Well, so much the better—it would be like old times, just the two of them talking and laughing far into the night.

Hurriedly stuffing her perishables into the refrigerator, Mary Kay mentally checked her schedule for next week. Two meetings and the award dinner—she could skip all of those. Get someone to take her turn at the hospital.... Oh, Evie, Evie, how good it will be to see you again ... it's been so long....

She had a sudden memory of Eve's face that last time, after the wedding, when Eve and Warner were taking the train to California. Seeing it now in her mind's eye, it seemed to her that a shadow fell on the happiness there.... Was there a look about the eyes, a certain vulnerability—? No, Eve had been radiant, then. She must be tuning in to Eve and picking up some passing anxiety of some kind. It often happened with the two of them.

She looked about the house and saw it as Eve would see it. If there were only time, she wished she could repaint the white brick of the fireplace and recover the sofa pillows. Well, never mind, they would be together again; that was all that mattered. Still in her stocking feet, she ran to the closet and began to check the guest linens.

It was seven years ago, in 1945, during the time Mary Kay and Eve were sharing an apartment on the Near North Side, that it all began. It had been one of those February evenings only Chicago could inflict. Mary Kay had just washed her hair and Eve was typing a letter at the table in the dinette when Sue, who lived down the hall, knocked at the door.

"Who is it?" asked Mary Kay.

"It's me—Sue. Bored to death— Jimmy broke our date—blames it on the storm—," Sue called out in her usual breathless, bouncy way, and as Mary Kay opened the door for her she continued, "so I thought if you two weren't busy, we could—guess what!" and she held up a Ouija board, with a flourish.

"Shut the door, Sue; the hall is cold and my hair is wet," Mary Kay said as she took the board from her and examined it.

"I saw one work at a party. It was a lot of fun, so I got one," bubbled Sue. "Ever seen one of these in action?"

"Yes, they tell your fortune."

"Well, it didn't at the party, at least I hope not—one girl asked how many children she would have and it said 66. But it was fun—let's try it."

Eve called out from the dinette, "Bring it in here, Sue; I'm through with the table."

"Oh, we don't need a table," replied Sue. "You sit facing one another and put it on your knees. Something about positive and negative," she added carelessly.

"No, it's better on a table. I saw one last summer and that's how they did it," offered Eve.

The board lay on the dinette table, its arched alphabet spreading invitingly. Eve and Sue, experts by virtue of having seen this game before, were touching with their fingertips the small, triangular planchette, which remained stationary, as though nailed in place.

"Maybe it's stuck," said Sue, pushing it around vigorously. It glided smoothly when pushed and stopped dead still again when the pushing ceased.

"Maybe it isn't here," ventured Sue, apologetically.

"What isn't here?"

"The Weegee," Sue replied haphazardly.

The three sat waiting, silently. Nothing happened.

"Mary Kay, you try it," offered Sue after a time.

"Mary Kay took Sue's place. Quite soon the planchette began to move in circles.

"Are you pushing it, Eve?" asked Mary Kay.

"No, are you?"

"It's the Weegee," Sue informed them authoritatively. "Ask it a question!"

A self-conscious silence fell.

"Is it still snowing?" Sue asked rather loudly, for lack of a better question.

The planchette moved slowly to the printed *Yes*.

"Let me ask!" Eve said excitedly. "Will I get a letter tomorrow?"

"No," answered the board.

"Are you really the Weegee?" asked Mary Kay.

Again the planchette swung to the printed *No*.

"What is a Weegee, anyhow?"

"G-O-T M-E," spelled out the planchette. Squeals of excitement greeted this sally. Sue scrambled for pencil and paper to note down the letters as the planchette pointed them out, and then to divide them into words and sentences as best she could.

"Will I get a raise this month?"

"Will you-know-who ask me for a date?"

"When will I get married?"

"One at a time!" Mary Kay cried. "How can he answer three questions at once?"

"Thank you," responded the board, the planchette moving steadily from letter to letter as the girls called them out to Sue.

"How do you know it's a he?" Sue asked.

"I don't know. It just feels like a he," retorted Mary Kay. "*Are* you a he?" she asked the board.

"I am no she," was the reply.

"But I mean, are you a man?"

"I am a ghost. Boo."

There was another chorus of squeals and laughter. "He sounds real!" Eve exclaimed. "It's fantastic!"

"Matter of life and death," the board spelled slowly.

"Life and death," laughed Sue. "I got news for you—you're dead already."

"More than you know," the board replied.

"You *are* dead, aren't you?" asked Mary Kay.

"Wish I were," replied the board.

"Oh? Aren't you happy up there?"

"Up where?"

"You know, up *there*," said Mary Kay delicately.

"No."

"Why not?"

"There is a trunk beside my bed," the board stated. This announcement, for some reason, sent the girls off into gales of laughter.

"It's no use," said the board disgustedly. But the planchette continued to move in circles.

"I don't think it's so funny," Mary Kay said presently. "I feel rather sorry for him."

"Oh, Mary Kay, don't be a wet blanket," protested Sue. "It's only a game."

"I know it," muttered Mary Kay, irritably.

"Come on, Weegee, tell me, Weegee," persisted Sue, coaxingly, "when am I going to get married?"

"How the hell would I know?"

A shocked silence followed.

"They don't swear up there, do they?" asked Eve in a small voice.

"Sometimes," the board answered her.

The mood had changed in the small dinette. Quietly, Eve asked, "Are you, then, a spirit?"

"Yes."

Mary Kay said soberly, "What is it about the trunk?"

"It's the same trunk from my room when I was little," was the reply.

"What's the problem?"

"My room was too small for it. It was right beside my bed. Had to climb over it to get in and out of bed. That was the problem then, and still is."

"But you are up there now," Mary Kay pointed out, reasonably.

The planchette moved quickly. "So is the trunk. Can't get rid of it."

"How did a trunk get up there?"

Promptly the board replied, "I remembered it so it turned up."

Eve said, "Look, couldn't you just picture it gone?" Her face was intent.

Sue was looking at them strangely. "I think I'd better be going," she said, getting to her feet.

Unhearing, Mary Kay asked earnestly, "Who are you? Tell us your name."

The planchette moved quickly and decisively from letter to letter: "My name is Max Melchior. I was killed in action in Germany in December of 1944...."

From that crude beginning blossomed the friendship between Max and the two girls that was to affect all of them deeply.

Max upset every image they had ever held concerning "spirits." His perfectly natural conversational tone, liberally laced with the slang expressions of his day, dispelled any ghostly quality which the girls had assumed to be a necessary corollary of communication with "the other side."

His distress seemed to stem not at all from remorse over earthly failings or fear of an Almighty God, but rather from such discomforts as loneliness and homesickness. His constant complaint was that he could not function in his new environment; nor was there, apparently, any source of help open to him. At first, he could not even control his whereabouts. Simply thinking of a place—whether city or room or field—placed him immediately there. For this reason, he was much with his old company, with whom he had spent the last weeks before his death. He rarely suffered from his wound while in conversation with the girls unless they reminded him of it. They learned very quickly to avoid subjects which would bring him pain.

That he was earthbound was obvious—even to two so uninitiated in the lore surrounding survival after death as were Eve and Mary Kay. His earthbound state gave them no little concern. They felt instinctively that Max should adjust to his new life, leaving the old behind. He admitted that this was so, but pointed out that he could hardly make an adjustment to a realm in which he could neither communicate nor stay in one place. Further, he was torn by the conviction that insanity, rather than death, might account for his situation; however, conversation with the girls seemed to give him temporary reassurance that his mind—if not his body—was intact. Their youth, their naiveté, and their matter-of-fact acceptance of him hardly had the ring of hallucination. Above all, their growing affection and solicitous interest warmed him.

Of his life before death he recalled little, and he seemed disinclined to discuss even that. Under questioning, he revealed that he "must have been about thirty-three" years of age when "it" happened; that he was rather tall; that he had green eyes and dark hair; and that he was Jewish. To the girls, he seemed to possess a singular sweetness—a dearness—along with the uninhibited sprightliness of his speech, which they found captivating. But it was his need of them that called forth a response which was new to them.

They had abandoned early any attempt to reconcile Max's condition with the implications of their religious training regarding life after death, and dismissed the problem. Max was clearly not in any orthodox heaven; on the other hand, unhappy as he was, his condition was not so severe as to resemble the orthodox hell. Certainly, death appeared to have transformed him into neither saint nor demon. Leaving these matters to religious theorists, Eve and Mary Kay concentrated on the immediate problem of finding ways for Max to survive his situation.

To the girls, Max's apparent lack of emotion about his mortal life meant that at least for the time being his earthbound condition resulted not from attachment to the old, but rather from lack of facility with the new. His feelings of loneliness and homesickness seemed to amount to little more than a yearning for familiar conditions. If this were true, the girls reasoned, his situation would improve as facility improved. Max agreed that he had to learn more about how to function in his strange environment. As weeks passed, he shared with them each effort to learn his way about the new world.

He was living with his grandmother, of whom he was

genuinely fond. He could converse freely with her, but hardly at all with the few friends who came to call on her. He told the girls that when he wanted to know why she lived such a solitary life, she had replied that after a long life in a crowded tenement, she valued her privacy. For Max, however, the small apartment was a prison. One evening when he had been complaining bitterly about this to Eve and Mary Kay, Eve suggested to him that he should have a home of his own.

"I wish I could," Max said.

"A little house, Max, with a small orchard behind it," Mary Kay offered impulsively.

"Yes, and a brook," added Eve.

The board and Max were silent for some time. Finally he said, "I can see it—the house, and all the rest—it's sitting over there!"

"You mean—like a picture?"

"Kind of."

"Do you like it?"

"No."

"Oh, Max," cried Mary Kay, "why not?"

"Who wants a house?" scoffed Max. "I never lived in a house."

"Well then, what would you like?"

And just so simply was the secret unlocked. Max began to describe the apartment he would like to have, and as he did so, it began to take form.

All that summer the three friends worked on the apartment for Max.

The girls had discovered fairly soon that while Max could create a visible and lifelike object by picturing it in his mind, the thought-form was not substantial enough to be of any use to him unless created and understood in great detail. Once successfully created, they found, the creation must have regular attention, if it were not to fade away. The offending trunk in Max's room at his grandmother's began to lose its form and substance as they forgot about it in their enthusiasm for the new dwelling place. And one evening Max told them that he had noticed that it was no longer there at all.

They were dismayed to find that following their animated discussion of the disappearance of the trunk, Max found it once more in place. At length they realized that they had all three combined forces to recreate the trunk by focusing their attention upon it. This was their first clue that Max could create something he did not want by the same process through which he could create a thing which he did want.

The enormity of this discovery was for a time overwhelming to them all. Not only must Max be prepared to live with such materialized mental pictures, whether desired or not, but it now appeared that Mary Kay and Eve could and did add their creations to his, and for this the responsibility was theirs. This sobering development caused the girls such anxiety that for a time they became almost reluctant to speak with Max through the board, or of him to each other, lest they create for him, or suggest to him, causing him to visualize, an unwanted object or condition. When the conversations resumed, all three were aware that discipline of thought was the factor which would determine to what degree Max would create his own heaven or his own hell.

Max's apartment and its furnishings became a special pleasure to the girls after their discovery that not only could they assist Max in his visualizations, but that they could also create gifts for him, gifts of their own devising. This enlarged the possibilities tremendously, since in the early stages of their adventure, they had thought Max's creative powers limited to that with which he was familiar. Now, they realized that they were not limited by Max's taste in home furnishings—which they considered deplorable—nor by financial or utilitarian considerations, but only by the scope of their own imagination. They were eager to press upon him all the appurtenances of which they could conceive.

"Max, you gotta have a chaise longue in front of the fireplace in your bedroom."

"Are you kidding? I got a fur rug in front of my fireplace. I don't need anything else."

"Well, for that matter, you don't *need* a fireplace. What have you got it for, anyway? To keep warm? No, you have it because you enjoy it. Same with the chaise, you'll learn to like it. An extra-long one, for your long legs. Covered in creamy white velvet. Like this, see?" Mary Kay closed her eyes and visualized the thought-form as clearly as she could.

"Well, okay," Max finally answered, the planchette moving slowly and reluctantly. "But not with that velvet cover. Too womanish. What about leather?"

"Sure, but only over my dead body."

In the end, Mary Kay yielded, and a leather-covered chaise longue was installed, before the fire, on the great, black fur rug. Months later, Max reported that he was using the chaise and enjoying it, and added that he guessed he was now ready for the velvet cover.

Caught up in the excitement of learning to manipulate his environment, Max improved rapidly. At what point he accepted the fact that he had indeed lost his physical body, the girls never knew. Possibly Max himself did not know. He mentioned no more his fear that he was insane, nor did any of them think any more of his wound. He seemed intensely curious about the workings of the natural laws to which he was now subject. His attitude had slowly changed from fear to bitterness, to lethargy, to mild interest, and on up the scale to enthusiasm. Eve and Mary Kay were amused when he began to compare his world with theirs in patronizing terms, like a gauche tourist in reverse.

The greatest advance of all came suddenly. Max told them one evening that he had had a visitor. "A tall guy with a yellow beard," Max described him, "who grinned at me and said, 'Well, Max old fellow, are you ready to talk?'"

With elation and wonder, he related the story of their evening together and of his visit to the stranger's house ("Some class!" said Max). With communication, Max's new life at last had reality for him. Eve, touched and tremulous with joy for her friend, asked, "Max, did he tell you his name?"

"Sure," replied Max. "It's Scott Allen."

Although the girls had felt from the beginning that Max communicated with them because he had no one else to talk to except Gramma and her friends, and although they regarded this as evidence of his lamentable earthbound condition, they were reluctant to give him up to his new life. Apprehensive lest their abiding affection become the chains with which he would be bound more firmly than ever to a world which should be receding from his view, they expressed their feelings to Max. To their relief, he replied matter-of-factly that Scott had instructed him that there was no reason why he should not have friends on both levels of consciousness, and further, that there was no reason why the girls should not do so, also, if they were capable of communicating.

He added, however, an observation of Scott's which gave them cause for much discussion. Scott had said that the evil in communication between the levels existed in direct ratio to the extent to which it prevented a full and vigorous involvement in the level to which one belonged at the time. After deciphering the meaning of this statement, the girls were reassured. It was abundantly clear that Max was wholeheartedly living his life in "one world at a time." His conversations with them now had the ring of long-distance telephone calls placed to old friends to report on his adventures from the center of *his* universe, not theirs.

As for Eve and Mary Kay, no question arose as to which world they belonged. Eve had met Warner on her vacation and they had fallen deeply and happily in love almost at once. Max, sharing her happiness, offered advice on honeymoon plans and brotherly instructions on how to handle a man. When asked what Scott thought of her approaching marriage, Max said that Scott had sent only the cryptic message, "Give them my blessing."

Mary Kay was giving up her job on the magazine and was going to Washington, D.C., to work on a newspaper there. They felt very close to Max as the time came for the girls to part. On their last evening with him his final words were, "Love you both. Don't forget to write."

Since the separation of Eve and Mary Kay had put an end to their joint effort at board communication, Max's life was now closed to them. They assumed, however, that he was continuing to observe their affairs with the same keen interest which he had always exhibited. Not long after Eve and Warner were married, Warner was transferred to the West Coast, where they had been established ever since. Eve, writing to Mary Kay, said that the designing and furnishing of their new home had proved to be such a period of happiness for her that she understood more deeply than before how Max had been rescued from his despair through the creative involvement with his apartment that summer.

Mary Kay met Kenneth Wilson at a dinner party in Washington, and they were married several weeks later. During the first months of marriage Mary Kay continued with her newspaper job, giving it up reluctantly only when the arrival of her first baby made it necessary. In those days she was intensely alive, so busy and happy that it often struck her as strange that she missed Eve and Max so very much.

The girls had kept up a rather lively correspondence, sharing their happiness, their changing values, their accomplishments and their plans. They spoke often of Max, at first with nostalgia and then with growing concern. Recalling Max's condition when they parted, the girls agreed that Max was clearly far enough along the road to a permanent adjustment so as to be in little danger of regressing to his early state, even though deprived of their supervision. At least in so far as they could tell, knowing as they did so little of the world Max lived in, his need for contact with them was probably not acute. This being the case, they admitted that they simply missed him—"miss him, miss him, miss him, my darling, sweet, funny angel-come-lately," wrote Mary Kay—and while they wished to hear more of his adventures, there did not seem to be any opportunity for their getting together to work the board.

Warner, during the time in Chicago when he and Eve were enjoying their courtship and engagement, had on many occasions witnessed the conversations between Max and the girls. His attitude had been one of tongue-in-cheek acceptance. Because it amused him to do so, he had treated Max with playful camaraderie, in the way one would treat a pet household spirit. Embarrassed, Eve had apologized to Max for her fiance's patronizing manner. Max had retorted cheerfully that he didn't give a damn one way or the other about the degree of Warner's acceptance.

"Oh, come on now, Max," Warner had laughed. "How come you can't rustle up a good tip on the stock market for an old pal? Seems to me it's a pretty inefficient ghost that can't produce even one little sure-thing. I'll bet you could if you tried."

"Sorry, pal. And I can't rattle chains, either."

Kenneth responded to Max in an entirely different way. While he had not seen any of their conversations, he was interested in Mary Kay's account of the friendship and its circumstances, and he questioned her at some length concerning Max's personality, purported experiences and background. But his particular interest seemed to be in the operation of the board itself. As a scientist, he shrugged off preconceived attitudes and felt only the desire for truth, caring little, if at all, what the truth turned out to be. His mind, already well-suited to research, was kept continually sharpened by his work in naval research and development. Mary Kay's experience, he knew, had to have an explanation. It was not in him to ignore it.

Having no proof that the board-writing must be done in tandem, Kenneth encouraged Mary Kay to experiment with operating alone. Only partial success resulted from the first months of her effort. Convinced that it was impossible to operate satisfactorily alone, she persevered mostly because of his urging. Slowly, however, the halting sentences took on clarity and meaning. The line was at last open to Max.

Max's account of his experiences over the years following their parting in Chicago was startling. Mary Kay and Eve had hoped for him only that he become comfortable in his environment and that he be relieved of loneliness and depression. They had expected him to continue to revel in his apartment, enjoying Scott's companionship and making new friends. But as Max's story came over the board, Mary Kay began to wish ardently that she were not operating alone. With someone to share the responsibility of producing such striking material, she would feel less inclined, perhaps, to question the validity of her work. For far from finding Max pursuing contentment and companionship within the lush confines of his habitation, she found him surrounded by hundreds of people, his time and energy so absorbed in alleviating their manifold difficulties that he had almost no attention left to contemplate his own state of being.

He was working within a military system of some sort, she gathered, since he used references to superior officers and to military discipline. He was now a Major, he told her with satisfaction. The details concerning the military set-up (which he did not supply) were outweighed by the voluminous reports he gave on his daily work. His own experience at the time of transition had convinced him that the existing methods by which this spirit army was handling its new arrivals (war casualties) were inadequate. He had worked for a new emphasis on proper techniques of supervising the men from the first moment of death through the period of adjustment. The program had been through a prolonged period of trial and error, innovation, modification, experimentation and evaluation, and at length results had justified the refined version of the program beyond Max's highest hopes. Eventually the methods, now standard, were applied so widely that Dr. Forbes had envisioned a hospital and rehabilitation center, designed to service not only military but civilian problem patients as well.

After the long and exacting process of creating this facility (the Center), the Board of Directors had appointed none other than Max Melchior as Chief of Staff. This piece of idiocy had shaken Max deeply. Although the original concept had been his, he knew that this in no way qualified him to administer such a stupendous program. He had envisioned himself with perhaps one company of volunteers doing what they could to alleviate transition trauma among such patients as they could. But Dr. Forbes had not been interested in such stopgap measures; instead, he had replied with his monumental proposal, the Center. In answer to Max's protests of inadequacy, even his lack of enthusiasm for the responsibilities Forbes planned to place upon him, Forbes explained that Max was still unaware of "the capabilities of the mind when freed from the demands of the flesh." He followed this observation with the statement that

Max was *required* to carry out the assignment, and to carry it out in a gratifying fashion at that, and that the discussion was at an end.

Mary Kay fumed at this. Max's reverence for Dr. Bixby Forbes left her unmoved. "He's a smug and self-satisfied tyrant, Max," she cried. "Where does he get off, bossing you around like that? You don't have to take that. Tell him to drop dead!" But Max, saying little or nothing further of Forbes, continued to revere and obey.

This was but one example of information about Max's life and the people who inhabited his daily world which raised Mary Kay's hackles. She longed for the days of the old Max, bewildered, dependent, sweet. This new Max she must learn to know. The more she heard of his life in his stern, strange world, the less she liked it. Still, fascinated, she could not turn away. She listened as Max spelled out, letter by letter, the story of his daily challenge, his victories, his defeats, his frustrations and his fears. No more the chummy conferences evolving into a lovely room, a gorgeous apartment. Max now poured out his situation to her daily, and nowhere was there room for humor or for any indication of personal happiness. Of the old Max, only his tenderness remained. Loving him, Mary Kay continued receiving his messages. Kenneth recorded them for her, separating the string of letters as they came through into words, and dividing the words into phrases and sentences (often by guess and surmise), punctuating them cavalierly and sometimes inaccurately. Nevertheless, his interest in her psychic work remained keen, although he made very little comment on the messages themselves.

Once only, he asked a question that grew out of

concern for Max. "I thought the dead were supposed to be happy and at peace, Max. How come you're always in some kind of a hassle?"

"Are you kidding? Who's happy, really, anywhere—except in rare moments, hours, days? Life is a hassle, your side, my side, the same, only different. On and on and on it goes, and where it stops nobody knows. They call it growth. I call it lifebah."

"What does he mean, Ken, *lifebah?*"

That was how Max's "Life—bah!" came to be a catchword with them.

IM-*level*

They lay comfortably before the fire, on the deep carpet. The room was dim; the sound of falling water came faintly from the bedroom fountain. Max turned lazily to look at Ida. She lay on her stomach, head on folded arms, and was regarding him steadily from far behind her swimming dark eyes.

"It's that you have to start reliving it at a time like this," she answered his unspoken question.

Max wiped rather clumsily at her tears with one finger. "Come on, Ida, cut it out."

Ida slapped viciously at his hand and sat up. "I think you like to wallow in it. I tune my death scene out whenever I feel it coming. Why can't you?"

"I'm sorry."

"No you aren't. You never are."

"Yes, I'm sorry to make you go through it every time."

"You are the one who goes through it, over and over. That's what I can't stand. I can't stand to watch it."

"I've told you—don't watch. Tune it out."

"You know I can't. And I've told *you*—if you picture it, I have to look, and you know it and you run it anyhow."

He was silent. Ida looked about the room, seeing the untouched supper table, her peacock robe across a chair.

"Just go," she told him, savagely. "Go home and run it by yourself."

He did not speak.

With a sigh, Ida moved close to him, holding him tightly. Her dark hair fell across his face and he left it there. She kissed him quickly.

"Okay, lover," she said, "roll 'em."

What a hell of a time to have to go to the latrine! Max wiped the sleet from his eyes, looking over his shoulder for Lieutenant Weber. Where were they all? Far ahead he could see them between the trees. They were dismantling a piece of equipment, it looked like. He tried to run. He could no longer distinguish their forms. Don't shout, he remembered, and he didn't try to. He could see the dripping black branches of the bare trees against the dark sky, and the sleet stung sharply on his upturned face. Had he fallen, he wondered? Must have. Cold mud was slipping down his neck. The inside of his pants felt hot and wet, but there was no pain any longer.

A voice came, strangely close to his ear. Familiar. Impossible. Nevertheless, it was. It was, because now he could see her plump little form and her beautiful white hair as she came toward him. "Oh Christ," he thought, panic racing through him, "I'm cracking up."

She stood there, looking down at him, gesturing vigorously. She was real, all right. "Gramma, for God's sake, get out of here!" he shouted. No, don't shout. Don't shout, men, not even when you're hit, if you can help it. Just don't holler.

"Now see what you made me do?" he said in a furious whisper. "You're going to get us both killed." He could smell his sweat as it ran across his cheeks and down his neck . . . and another smell . . . what?

Now he could hear what she was saying. "Maxie," she ordered crossly, "get up out of that mud. A cold you want? Come here to me."

She pulled him to his feet. He stood, with difficulty, leaning on her . . . how short she was.

"Machile, I'm telling you for your own good, you died completely from the hole in your insides. You got a lot of surprises in front of you."

Nothing is real. . . .

Holding his arms across his belly, he doubled over. The pain was returning. Suddenly his vision blurred as a hoarse scream rose to his chest and clawed at him, silent, choking. At his feet lay the dead body of a soldier. The face stared sightlessly into the sky. Sleet was beating against the unprotected eyeballs. The uniform, blood-soaked and wet with mud, gave him no clue. It was the hands that he recognized first, even before the face. *His* hands.

Fallen to his knees over the body, Max tried to close the eyes with his fingers, but he could not move them. He looked at the dog tag—"Captain Maxwell Paul Melchior"—no, it was only a number, not a name.

"Gramma," he called to her, "help me up."

It was not a gradual fading away when the wet woods disappeared. They were simply in another place. The room looked like Gramma's bedroom always looked.

"Sleep, Machile, and then I'm fixing you up," she said briskly as she turned down the covers. When she kissed him, she was substantial enough. It's a dream. I will rest and wake up. I'm just having a nightmare.

So it was. Nightmare, yes. But dream, no.

He had never thought much about life after death. The streets of gold were a Christian idea, for one thing. And not too appealing, for another. What *did* Jews believe about it? If he had ever know, he could not remember now. He was vague about parts of his life before he got in this condition. Whatever he might have been taught, it wouldn't have done any good now. This was something no one could be prepared for. He had seen no one but Gramma since it happened, and she was no help. She acted as if it was all perfectly normal. She said he was dead, but God, it didn't make sense. What kind of a way was this to be dead?

No, it was more likely to be shock. He knew all the symptoms of shock. He'd seen plenty of it in combat. Including hallucinations. All kinds of hallucinations, visual, auditory, you name it. And he had every damn one of them. Just have to wait, that's all. It will wear off.

The trembling began again, and the pain of his wound made him weak. Insanity. That was the most logical of all.

Gramma came into the room carrying a candlestick.

She put it on the small table beneath the window and smiled companionably at him. "It's sundown, Maxie. In here I'm lighting the candles so you can see."

"What for, for God's sake?" cried Max. "Whatta ya, trying to make everything spooky?"

"No, Machile, it's the Sabbath. The candles I got to light."

Max felt his control slipping. "Stop talking to me!" he shouted hysterically.

Gramma came to the bed and wiped his face firmly with a small towel. "He yells at an old woman," she said, addressing the ceiling, "but I excuse."

Max caught her around the waist, burying his face against her. "Gramma . . ." He felt the hot tears wetting her dress. She held him, saying nothing. "Gramma," he groaned, "this is hell."

Ida seized his face fiercely between her hands. Even in the dim light she could see that his eyes were wet.

"Stop it, Max. That's enough. Stop it now. Hush, darling. Look, Max, it's me." She pulled him to a sitting position. He was quiet now and looked at her vaguely.

Ida knelt beside him, holding him. He was still trembling slightly. "It's over now, goddammit," she urged, her voice rising. "All that was years and years ago. You found the way out. It's just a memory. So don't torture yourself any more."

"Stop yelling at me," said Max in a normal voice. "Listen, I want to ask you something; why is it you holler so much, anyway?" Getting to his feet he pulled her up. Holding her body very gently, he whispered into her hair, "Why is it you yell at me all the time?"

Ida, her face against his, closed her eyes with relief.

"Maybe my hot Latin blood?" she murmured shakily. Latin blood, yes, good enough match any day for his stupid dumb Bronx Brooklyn Jerseyshore wherever it was he came from lovetalk, his murmuring, nuzzling ... that's right, Max darling ... doesn't have to be poetry ... what did that poet say, comfort me with honey ... ?

But in the night she knew he could not sleep. Baby, she thought, my poor baby. Curving her body to his she began patting him. After a time she thought he slept. Loving this guy was no picnic, she mused drowsily, but it's worth it.

Ida arose with the first light, leaving Max sleeping quietly in her wide bed. He lay with his face turned aside, showing the rich deep color of his cheeks and the clipped black beard against the apricot pillow.

"You are gorgeous," she said to him silently. He stirred slightly and she tuned out instantly so as not to disturb him further.

Dressed and ready for the office, she recorded a note to him before she left the room: "I'm going in early, to process last night's lists before you get there. Flash my department when you wake up. Hope you slept well. You kept me awake all night, rat."

Leaving her house she flashed her houseman, Wilmer. He answered sleepily.

"Tune in on Major Melchior in my bedroom and when he wakes up see if you can get him to eat something. I'm going to the office."

She projected straight to her own office. No one was about, since she rarely arrived this early. Good, she could pull her aura together a bit before Bertram came. Seated at her cut-glass and silver desk she leaned back for a moment in the rose velvet chair. Bertram—she would have to do something about Bertram soon. She pushed the thought away with determination. Picking up the communicator, she flashed. Robert answered at once.

"Good morning, Miss Adriano."

"Robert, is Eve still there?"

"She went back about two-thirty this morning, M-time."

"Well, I have to check on that girl Max sent home with Scott. Is he available?"

"I'm sorry, he is not. He is at the Archives. Would you care to flash him there?"

Ida deliberated. "How is the girl by now, Robert?"

"She is having coffee in the garden—"

"Drinking it? Or throwing it?" queried Ida, somewhat startled.

"—and partaking liberally of iced melon and rolls," added Robert, smoothly.

Suddenly suspicious of his rather smug tone, Ida demanded, "Alone?"

"No, Madam."

"Then who—?"

"Your humble servant, Madam."

"Listen, Robert," Ida said, faintly alarmed, "I want that girl in Major Melchior's office by ten o'clock. And you'd better come along," she added, "and stop calling me Madam."

"Thank you, Madam."

Ida cut off the beam abruptly. The day was starting on the wrong tone. She would get tired if this irritability continued. Firmly she cleared it from her aura and projected to Max's office. The night lists lay on his desk.

She took her place in his chair, feeling his vibration lingering there. Her throat tightened with a sudden onrush of emotion. Resolutely, she dispelled that, too, and settled down to work.

Carrying a small tray of supper, Robert tapped lightly on Harriet's door, and entered without waiting for her reply. The girl was lying face down upon the rumpled bed, and gave no sign that she was aware of his presence. Noting the deep indigo hue in the center of her aura, he set the tray down. She would not be able to eat while her depression was so deep.

"Harriet," he said firmly, "sit up. I want to speak to you."

Harriet did not move. Following Max's instructions, Robert grasped her carefully, turning her body very slowly and gently until she faced him, her shoulders suspended in his arms. Great grey eyes stared at him, unseeing.

"Harriet, come back. Come here. Come here at once." He focused intently on her, boring through the murky light about her, probing for her attention.

"Robert?" she said at last. "They are all at my funeral. I saw it. All of it."

"You were there, Harriet. That's why I had to bring you back."

"I can't stand this, Robert," she moaned, sagging in his arms. "Nobody could stand it. I'm going to crack up. I don't know what happened. I don't know why I'm here. I don't even know how I got here. I know I'm dead. I can tell I'm dead." Her hands reached for his face, holding his cheeks, her eyes close to his. "I don't even know how it happened, how all of a sudden I got to be dead, do you hear that?" she shouted.

Hastily, Robert stood her on her feet, supporting her against his own body. Keep her attention, Max had said. Do anything necessary to prevent the death-memory. It's much too soon for her to ...

"Harriet, Harriet!" he cried, over her screams. He propelled her forward but she could not walk. In panic, he shook her, hard, but she seemed not to notice.

He flashed frantically for Max, for the hospital, for anyone, but he could not tell whether there was a response.

She had stopped screaming now and hung limply, awkwardly, in his arms. Her face so near his own was no longer the freshly rounded face of youth, the full lips were stretched across her teeth in a macabre grimace, and on the pallid cheeks lay an acrid dew. Pity seized him, pity as for a wounded bird or a small animal ensnared within a cruel trap.

He placed his open palm beneath her head and lifted, so that it would not hang so heavily upon the fragile neck. His fingers spread deep within her heavy hair. Her eyes lay black-fringed, closed to him. Without warning, there swept throughout his being an unutterable longing. It was a yearning so piercing that his force flowed from him as from a mortal wound. The centuries of wise and cautious living, the small and simple pleasures, the gentle satisfactions which had always been enough but never, never too much—all were now obliterated in this wash of unaccustomed feeling. Incredulous, he saw his own tears had fallen on her upturned face.

When she began to stir, he did not at first believe it. With the most unspeakable tenderness he had ever known, he kissed her hair. When he did so, she pushed irritably against him.

"Leave me alone, for heaven's sake!" she complained in a perfectly normal voice. "Honestly, this is the weirdest place in the world. What are you doing, anyway, making over me like that? You leave me alone, you—you spook, you!"

As one drowning, Robert registered her words, saw the reassuring crimson flares sparking from her auric rim. With tremendous relief, he stifled his desire to laugh aloud. Picking up the tray, he offered it with a show of casualness. "Have some hot soup, Harriet," he suggested, shakily.

"And get that spook soup away from me, too," she shrilled, knocking it out of his hand. In confusion, Robert began to mop at the spilled soup with the napkin.

"And stop messing with that spook carpet! Everything in this place is spook. Nothing is real. Spook houses! Spook trees! Spook food! And spook talk, and spook people, and spook kisses! It isn't even Heaven! I can't stay here!"

Robert fixed her with a stern gaze, his thoughts unspoken. Harriet, her eyes not leaving his, stopped shouting.

"Yes, Robert," she admitted finally, "I'm a spook, too."

The communicator glowed and almost absently Robert picked it up.

"What's going on out there?" queried Max. "Nobody's been answering my flashes."

"I know."

"Well, how is the patient? What's she doing now?"

"She just threw a cup of soup on the floor."

"Good," laughed Max. "She's mad again. I see you've kept her attention."

Sitting cross-legged upon the bed, Harriet regarded the supper tray with distaste. Her face, still tear-ravaged, was flushed.

"I'm not hungry," she protested. "I don't see why you keep bugging me to eat."

"Because you must sustain your body."

"You said it's a spirit body. Why does a spirit body need to eat food?"

"A spirit body must be supplied with energy, Harriet. The only means of sustenance you are familiar with is the intake of food and drink. Later, you will understand how to maintain your body without food, if you choose to do so, but for the time being you must survive, using methods which are instinctive."

"But you eat. All the other spooks eat, too. They are forever drinking coffee. And they drink booze, too. Haven't they learned not to need all that?"

"Some of us have learned. However, these functions are deeply associated with enjoyment. For that reason, as well as for sustenance, we continue to create pleasures such as these."

"You mean you eat because you like to? And that goes for other things as well?"

"And other things, as well."

Handing the tray to Robert, Harriet rose from the bed and began to walk slowly about the room, thinking. Robert watched carefully, observing the steady flow of the aura. The flickering and the flashing had ceased. For a moment, pity stirred him. How young she was, to pass through this bewildering change! On the other hand, he reminded himself, her youth would be an advantage to her in many ways, one of which being that she would accept a new environment more readily than was often the case with the rigid elderly.

What was she dwelling upon just now, he wondered, as he watched her standing at the window, her back to him, absently toying with the strands of her disordered hair? He sought to intercept her thoughts, but she had closed herself into privacy.

At length she turned to him, her eyes wide. "You know something, Robert?" she said tremulously. "I really don't know what I was expecting. Well, I mean, I wasn't expecting it ... you know ... I didn't think about it much. All I knew, I took it for granted that Jesus would be here."

"He is."

"Then why haven't I seen him?"

"You haven't thought of him. That is the reason."

"But he was supposed to be waiting."

"He is waiting."

"You mean I will see him?"

"If you really want to, yes, you will see him. Do you want to?"

"Yes. Well ... actually, I'm not really sure. I just thought he'd be here, you know, anytime anyone gets here."

"He is not one of the local tourist attractions, Harriet. If you come to desire it, deeply, you will see him."

She was silent a moment. Then, "Not right now ..." she said.

"There is plenty of time," smiled Robert. "Just now, I must insist that you try to eat something."

"Oh, Robert," she said petulantly, flouncing into a large armchair, "I just can't. I don't like that stuff you brought me. It has a weird sauce on it. I don't even know what it is."

On more comfortable ground now, Robert stood up. "Let me get you something else," he urged enthusiastically. "What would appeal to you?"

"Just a hamburger, that's all."

"I beg your pardon?"

"You know—a hamburger. And french fries and a large coke."

Crestfallen, Robert sat down again. "I don't recognize any of those items," he admitted reluctantly. "I cannot create them if I do not know them. Perhaps I can find someone who is familiar with them to provide them."

"Wait a minute, Robert. Are you saying you never heard of a *hamburger*?"

"Never."

"And you don't know where to get one?"

"I'm sorry, no."

"For heaven's sake, it's no big deal. A hamburger is a meat patty with . . . well, first you have to have a bun."

"Yes, a bun. I know what that is."

"This big round bun, see, about this big," and she demonstrated with her hands.

"With icing or without?"

"*Icing?*" exclaimed Harriet incredulously. "Wow, Robert, you're not even trying! Look. See, you take this bun, and it's not sweet, it's like a dinner roll, only big." She was leaning forward, gesturing, her face earnest. Robert saw it before Harriet did, for her eyes were on his face. On one outstretched palm reposed the bun, fresh and golden brown. When Harriet saw it she almost dropped it.

"You see, Harriet, what you have accomplished?" cried Robert exuberantly. "You have produced a bun by imagizing it with great detail."

When Harriet could speak, she muttered to herself, "But I wanted one with seeds on top."

Robert laughed in spite of himself. "Then give it seeds!" he cried out triumphantly. "Come, Harriet, show me the seeds!" And unable to restrain himself, he pulled her to her feet and kissed her cheek.

Harriet's eyes were bright, her little face intent. Holding her hamburger bun tenderly in both hands, she said to it, "Whatever kind of seeds that was, that were on the ones we used to get on Friday nights at the Hamburger Heaven..."

Joel Higgins leaned back in his chair and placed his heavy portfolio upon the conference table. The staff meeting had been in progress for some time and now that department reports were in, various decisions made, and some assignments given, it would soon be time for him to present the Instructions from the Planning Group, the Instructions that were the crucial content of every staff conference.

Today, concerning one case, he was deeply disturbed. Not for the first time in the many years he had occupied the position of Liaison Officer (the link between the august Planning Group and the staff) he asked himself whether he could continue in the job. Only his devotion to Dr. Forbes, head of the Foundation, had enabled him to preserve his emotional integrity throughout the resolution of several heartbreaking cases. Was he to be put to the test again?

His thoughts turned loyally to that great man of science and humanity, Dr. Bixby Forbes. Objective, desireless, dedicated completely to the eternal viewpoint, Dr. Forbes had long since ignited in Higgins a consecrated fire. Dr. Forbes' genius was focused upon the achievement of spiritual progress in man through the improved efficiency of the reincarnation process. Forbes had recognized the fact that reincarnation had been, for many thousands of years, a tragically hit-or-miss affair—impulsive, compulsive, misused, abused, and subject to mishaps of astronomical number. He knew that, generally speaking, candidates for incarnation simply did not have the necessary data for optimum planning of their next trip. It was this that Dr. Forbes had determined to remedy, by any and all means possible. Higgins, inspired by the potential of Dr. Forbes' work, had years ago become his ardent disciple. In fact, Higgins chuckled to himself, Ida Adriano frequently referred to Dr. Forbes and himself as "Christ and the Apostle Paul." He had, of course, publicly protested this appellation, but had secretly relished the analogy.

His was the most thankless job in the entire Foundation, Higgins complained to himself as the voices in the room continued to hum around him. The Planning Group, those Invisible Ones from the Higher Plane (so irreverently referred to by the staff as "Upstairs"), with their marvelous access to total recall and to precognition, were able to assess both the past and the future and to use this knowledge to map out efficiently a plan for the future incarnation of each candidate, to whom it was duly offered. What a supremely significant service, thought Higgins, to give assistance in moving a life more truly in the direction of the one and only goal, spiritual progress! One would expect deepest gratitude and utmost cooperation from the recipient. But, he mourned, people tend to cringe from the sacrifices so often necessary to effect growth in their own basic selves, or in others. The precious Instructions from the Group, obtained only by his own scrupulous psychic work, often brought forth storms of protest, and the blame more often than not was visited upon him, personally. "I am only the courier," he frequently defended himself (the Apostle?).

Still, this particular case, today, distressed him. The mortal Eve, so understandably planning to join Scott permanently, must be told the truth—that her contract forbid it. She had not yet fulfilled the purpose for which she had re-entered the physical world. Her contract was with a child who was not yet born.

He should not become emotionally involved with the clients. Dr. Forbes had always stressed that point. However, admitted Higgins, he had not yet achieved perfection, and so he had—against his better judgment—permitted an attachment to grow between himself and Scott Allen. Sympathy for Scott and Eve in their long separation welled suddenly in his chest. His eyes filled.

Reaching into his portfolio, Higgins extracted the memorandum to Scott and he placed it in his breast pocket. He could, at least, put it off. For a little while yet, let them hope.

Bertram had left the clinic early. He had thought to go directly to his quarters to rest and recharge before his evening lecture. He would be speaking on one of his favorite subjects, "The Anatomy of Consciousness," and he looked forward to it with a sense of exhilaration. He wished to deliver the lecture with great force and clarity and to illustrate it with powerful thought-images of his own creation; all this would require a deep supply of vital force. Moreover, there would be a large audience, and there would be many questions—and doubtless some hostility, since his subject was a controversial one—and he must provide for himself a protective shield to prevent possible psychic burn from antagonists. As he left the clinic, however, he found his thoughts attracted to the river. He made his way slowly past the cathedral and the market plaza, along the avenue of fountains, to the great bridge which spanned that mighty stream.

The water far below was dark, yet shadowed darker still as the late afternoon light cast on its surface the shapes of buildings which lined its banks here in the city. Far out of sight, he knew, it flowed past grasslands; farther still, through forests.

Bertram liked this vantage point upon the bridge the best of all. He leaned upon the parapet, feeling the low surge of force which emanated upward from the water and he opened his aura to permit its rays to reach the central core.

George Bertram was a slender man of medium height. His jacket, opened from the sweater which he wore beneath it, was of a loose and indistinctive cut, giving him an appearance of youth in contradiction to his bearing. His rounded face, as well, belied the lines of strain about his mouth.

He had been a dweller in this immortal city for a

span of roughly eighty years. No one knew for certain when he had come, or how, exactly, he had taken leave of the mortal plane, because he never said how it had happened. Only his intimates knew that George was his Christian name. He, like so many others—particularly those who felt the minimum of interest in their mortal years and had no wish to perpetuate that identity—preferred to be designated by a single name.

Bertram turned his thoughts to consider the coming lecture: the nuclear pattern of the personality as well as of the basic self; the attraction of identities that are held in orbit around a male-female nucleus, repeated to infinity.... His attention wandered....

He recalled suddenly and with a stab of poignancy an occasion on which he had sat alone with Dr. Forbes on a warm evening, enjoying the early darkness and the view of the lighted city from the terrace of Dr. Forbes's home. It was a time not long before the great man had made his decision to leave this level, and this evening his dwelling and its environs reflected the power and beauty of his state of development ... all gone, all dissolved, of course, in the time since he had gone and there had been no support remaining, in the form of attention and appreciation, to maintain it all.

"My boy," he had said to Bertram, "you do not choose. You must be chosen. Being chosen, only then do you face the decision whether you will accept."

"Who chooses one, if that's the case?" Bertram had asked.

"Ah, Bertram," the doctor had replied, "I cannot tell you where the choice originates. We have our theories, our opinions, about the next level, but who can say precisely how the laws operate in that more rarified atmosphere? Wherever the choice is made, at least one way it is made known to us is through the body of Higher Ones we call the Planning Group. There are many other avenues, of course, through which the call can come."

"And if one refuses the call? What then?"

"Oh, it will come again. And yet again, if one refuses. We are perpetually drawn, I think. The door is never closed."

Bertram deliberately turned his attention away from the throbbing memory. The excitement had gone out of his anticipated lecture. He saw himself on the podium earnestly and endlessly presenting intellectual ideas to an audience which heard him in varied degrees of comprehension.

He turned and left the bridge.

Bertram lived alone in a two-room flat on the second floor of the clinic. The suite overlooked the formal garden and reflecting pool on the east side of the Education wing. Since he had relinquished his responsibilities at the Department of Minds Analysis to Ida Adriano, his former assistant, he had been devoting most of his attention to teaching and to the supervision of research. With the remaining energy he was able to summon, he was preparing a textbook for publication.

The rooms mirrored his singleminded dedication to his work. They were spacious rooms, one in which he slept and spent his rest and recharge periods, furnished with a simple cot and little else. His workroom was dominated by a large desk, the work stacked neatly on its top and in piles beside it on the floor. About the room stood cabinets holding his equipment. The recording device, the reproduction device which made his words visible as he composed, and three communicators of varied types were in this room. One of the communicators was glowing as Bertram returned to the flat.

"Hi, doll," said Ida's voice. "Max isn't going to make it to your lecture. Some emergency over at Admissions."

"I'm sorry to hear that," replied Bertram. "What about you?"

"Oh, I'm coming," she said. "But listen. What are you doing after? Can you come over to my place? Scott's coming and some other people and Max, if he gets away in time."

"What's the occasion?" asked Bertram, smiling at her tone of enthusiasm.

"Just a little party, that's all."

"In honor of Max's promotion?"

"No, not that. He says he's not accepting a change, anyhow."

"What, then?"

"Look, Bertram. Nobody needs to know it, I'd be embarrassed ... but, oh, I can trust you, love, but nobody else is to know ... just a plain supper party, y'know. But between you and me, I'm celebrating the anniversary of my homecoming."

"Ida!" said Bertram. "You are *not*, tell me you are *not*, going to celebrate—even inwardly—the worst trauma in your conscious memory!"

"Oh, don't be prim, Bertram. Everybody does it. But no one ever offered to commemorate mine, so I'm doing myself the honor."

"A barbarous custom, restimulating the transition experience! You should know better."

"Oh, Bertram," laughed Ida. "It's just like a birthday party on the mortal level. Birth is a trauma, too, but nobody is celebrating the trauma when they cut the cake. It's the years of life. Same with homecomings."

"Sometimes. Not always. Studies show that homecoming anniversaries produce a high percentage of depression and psychic accident."

"Oh, for God's sake, Bertram! It's the attitude. Listen, are you coming or not?"

"That depends. Are you having a cake?"

"Of course not. Don't be silly."

"In that case, I shall be delighted."

Later, gathering his materials for the lecture, he realized that his depression had lifted. He left the building and began to move briskly toward the auditorium.

As if to dispel any suspicion that this was a festive occasion, Ida was wearing a demurely simple white silk dress swinging above her tan legs, and low sandals. She was sitting curled in a large armchair in conversation with a renowned composer of opera and symphony. He sat on the thick carpet, one arm across the lap of his wife, a popular speaker on subjects relating to the production and preservation of vital force, mana.

"The entire concept is in error," she was saying to Ida. "We have to get the concept of mana as a stream flowing through us, from the Source, through us and on out, wherever we direct it. Our use of it should be a stewardship, actually. But that's what the public won't accept."

"I don't blame them," said Ida. "I don't like that idea myself."

"Why not?" asked the composer. "It doesn't diminish the individual one iota to accept the cosmic stream."

Bertram turned to listen to the discussion taking place on the sofa across the low table.

"Nothing but a myth," Scott was saying to the author sitting beside him. "Pure and simple myth. The records are there but the problem is that they are recorded by individual finite minds. There is no omnicient oversight of it."

"My dear fellow," protested the author. "You don't propose to advance such a postulate in your book?"

"I am not a novice," replied Scott, smiling. "I shall merely raise the question."

Max leaned across the table from his seat beside Bertram. "Why not say it, Scott?"

"I shall indeed say it, in good time."

"And there's plenty of time, is that it?" Max set his champagne glass on the table with a smart snap. "You want to know the whole lousy trouble with this whole lousy level? Time. There's too damn much time ahead. Nobody feels any urgency."

At Max's outburst the others had broken off conversation and were listening in surprise.

"Maxie," said the public speaker, "I felt that way too, for a long time. For me it passed, eventually."

"Oh, it passed, did it, Doc?" he said to her. "Great! So now you don't **suffer** any more from a sense of urgency!"

"Max," protested the composer, gently, "I must remind you—"

"Doc knows I didn't intend any impertinence. I've known her longer than you have."

"It's all right, darling," said Doc. "Go ahead, Maxie."

"I asked if now you have no urgency."

"Right," said Doc. "Only courage."

Bertram lifted his hand. "May I interject a thought?" he asked. "Did you ever wonder whether the trouble is not entirely a matter of there being too much time ahead, but rather of there having been too much time in the past? Myself, for an example. It has struck me of late that I have been engaged in various aspects of the same work for seventy years."

"That's another thing," Max's voice was rising. "The time past. Take a look at our staff. People who came to this level bringing over from the M various concepts dating all the way from the pre-Freudian era on up—including every whistlestop along the way. And we're supposed to operate—skillfully, yet!—out of this mishmash of philosophies, prejudices, biases, plain old superstitions and God knows what else.... We need to take a good clear look at the whole system. A complete reorganization, at the very least. In a word, reform!"

"Dear boy," said the author. "Aren't you waxing a bit radical?"

"Radical, hell," retorted Max. "I'm no radical. I'm a fanatic."

"And guilty of a cliché, as well," returned the author.

Ida sprang to her feet and hurried out of the room. Bertram followed her to the service area where she began to arrange sandwiches upon a tray. He saw that she was blinking back tears.

"I'll give you another cliché," she said, as he approached and put his hand on her shoulder. "This is the cliché, my pet: I'm not having a good time."

Bertram put both arms around her.

"Many happy returns!" he whispered in her ear.

"All right, what's the matter?" Ida demanded after the other guests had taken their leave.

"Nothing we have to talk about tonight," replied Max. He was slouched in a chair, staring moodily at the floor. "Maybe I'm tired. Let's let it go till later."

"What later?" said Ida. "When do you ever have time, lately? You complain about there being too much time in 'Summerland' but there's never enough time to suit you, yourself."

"Stick around," said Max, without raising his eyes, "it's going to get worse."

"What worse? What's happened? See, I knew you were in a snit."

"No mere snit, my pretty," responded Max. "I am, to use Scott's phrase, profoundly exercised. You could even go so far as to say I'm shook up."

"I'll go that far. Maybe even farther if you don't tell me why you're being so impossible."

"Well, I've accepted the directorship. Is that enough?"

Ida scrutinized him carefully. "I can see by your aura," she said, "that you are terribly angry. Why?"

"Because I'm forced into a position I don't want to be in. Isn't that reason enough? I can't stand being controlled."

"Nobody's controlling you. You can say no."

"I can't say no! And before you ask why, I'll tell you. It's because if I don't take the job I know who's next in line, a reactionary of the first rank. He would set Forbes' program back a half-century."

"But why—"

"Listen, I can't talk any more."

"So don't talk," Ida said. "Just hold me a minute till I get over being mad."

"Don't be mad," he said, looking at her. "Not on your homecoming day."

"You remembered all along! So why did you spoil my party?"

"Congratulations, baby," he said. "I guess I don't make it easy, do I?"

Ida curled in his lap, pressing her cheek against his lips. "You're never easy, lover," she said. "Don't try to be. Just be you." Her mouth moved to cover his. "Forever, Max. Stay Max forever."

Ida had worked steadily through the morning, checking reports on the cases her department had been assigned. Obviously, her seminar on regression techniques had borne fruit, for her staff was now reporting a gratifying upswing in the number of recalls produced by patients. And increasingly, patients were being reported ready for temporary suspension of therapy. Now, however, she held in her hands a report which troubled her. The patient had passed through Receiving without undue difficulty and had been transferred to her department, Minds Analysis, because of a mild depression which should have yielded to treatment quite readily. The report, signed by the analyst, was initialed by Bertram. The analyst had consulted Bertram about the case, which was proper procedure. What was it, then, which disturbed her? Was it the case itself? No, for whatever the nature of the problem the patient might have had, Bertram was perfectly capable of handling it. She opened her receptive center, seeking intuitive data. *It is Bertram himself, not the patient,* came the certainty. And following that thought came another thought, less definite, but intensely distressing.

With considerable alarm, she reached for the communicator and flashed Bertram's office. "Ask Mr. Bertram if he will come up to my office," she said to the secretary.

"He's out of the office, Miss Adriano."

"Where can I flash him?"

"He is in the meditation room," was the faintly reproving answer.

Ida considered. Bertram was spending a helluva lot of time in the meditation room lately. Daily meditation was a regular part of the working day, of course, but Bertram was overdoing it. "Go get him out of there and ask him to come up here," she said crisply.

"Miss Adriano . . ."

Ida picked up a vibration of concern, even compassion.

"I think I ought to see you, too," she told the secretary, thoughtfully. "Can you come up before closing time?"

"Of course."

Waiting for Bertram, Ida decided to send for his medical file. When it appeared on her desk screen she scanned the recent entries quickly. Fibrillation had been noticed in the inner aura, and a low intensity. Before she was able to finish her scan, Bertram appeared, his sensitive face looking strangely vulnerable.

"Hi, doll," she said to him, rising and pulling up a

chair for him. "You and I are getting ready to lock horns. Have you had lunch?"

"I had something a little while ago, thanks."

"Well, I haven't. Let's take time out. I'll get the waiter."

"Nothing for me, Ida," said Bertram, settling himself in the chair somewhat wearily.

"Listen, Bertram," said Ida testily, "I'm going to tell you something. You're no damn fun anymore. In fact, you've been a pain in the neck lately."

"You mean—just because I don't want lunch—?"

"Yes. You always used to want lunch. Or a glass of champagne. Or a concert with Max and me. Or a party. You've always been fun. But lately—I just don't know what's wrong with you lately."

"Is that why you've got my medical report on the screen?" he smiled wryly. "Is that what you got me out of meditation to tell me?"

"And that's another thing—," began Ida. But the waiter appeared just then, and she subsided in her chair.

"We would like some lunch ..." she told the waiter vaguely. A silence fell. Puzzled, the waiter hesitated. Ida waved one hand toward Bertram in annoyance. "See, Bertram, what a wet blanket you are? Now I can't even think what to order. Just bring us what we usually have on Mondays," she said to the waiter, "only bring some sherry first." The waiter retired hastily.

Ida sat regarding Bertram steadily, her hands clasped before her on the desk top.

"Dear friend, my Rock of Gibralter, I am going to ask you a question and you have got to level with me."

Bertram did not meet her gaze.

"Listen, Bertram, dammit, I've got to know." Her

voice broke. "Have you been contacted by the Planning Group?"

"Ida, if I had, you know I wouldn't be allowed to discuss it."

"Allowed, hell!" exclaimed Ida. "This is different. You taught me everything. If you went away— Without you—"

Bertram reached across the desk and took both her hands in his. "Darling child," he said, trying to smile; and then, "Here is our waiter with the sherry."

At the end of the day, Ida, waiting for Bertram's secretary, leaned back in her chair, eyes closed in concentration. She had worked during the afternoon under a crushing fatigue. Negative emotions always produced this enervation; she was careful not to indulge them if she could avoid it. This time, however, she had found self-discipline inadequate, and knew she must seek help outside herself. She sent out a request for mana. But this time, the familiar surge of quiet strength was not forthcoming. She started to ask the reason why, then almost at once answered her own question: God would not minister to her need while she still burned with defiance and bitterness.

She made a half-hearted attempt to cleanse her aura, but immediately admitted to herself that she had no intention of relinquishing her resentment any time soon. The entire system of reincarnation was thoroughly repellent to her. When she had first arrived on this level, she had been for some time totally unable to accept its reality. In conflict with the religious concepts which she had brought with her from the M-level, it remained an altogether appalling proposition.

In the entry now appeared Bertram's secretary of many years, looking tired and a little resentful.

"Come in, Rose," Ida said warmly. "I'm worn out, too. This won't take long. I'll come to the point. I think I've caught on to what's happening."

Rose's face wavered. She sat down, saying nothing.

"Look, Rose," Ida leaned across the desk. "Has Joel Higgins been in your office lately?"

"Twice in the last few days."

"Uh huh," said Ida reflectively. "Well, I want you to know I am filing a protest report with the Planning Group. Under the law, no decision can be made until all protests are considered."

Rose smiled in momentary relief. "I wasn't sure how you'd feel about it," she said frankly. "Having him go away, I mean. Now that you are the department head."

"Rose," said Ida, taking her hand across the desk, "do you remember when I first came here as a patient? What I was like? I was completely self-centered, spoiled, bound up with the M-level and all those things I had been torn away from. I was half-crazy with grief for all that I was bereaved of—my fiance, a boy I was mad about; my career, that I was just getting a toe-hold in; everything that mattered was ended for me, and I was convinced that I was doomed to an eternity of nothingness. You know how Bertram took my case himself. How he gave me a reason for existence here, by bringing me into this work. You know what the department means to Bertram, and I hope you know what it means to me. I'm not *ready* to carry the department without him."

"But you've been doing very well with it. It had

occurred to me that that's the very reason he might think it's time for him to release it."

"Listen, Rose. At the time he turned the department over to me, I knew I wasn't able to cut it without him, and so did he. I only accepted it with the understanding that I'd have him to turn to. I'm not going to stand for having the Planning Group take him away."

"Oh, now, you know they won't 'take him away.' He would have to agree to their proposal," protested Rose.

"I know," said Ida firmly, "and I intend to try to prevent him from agreeing."

"I've thought of that, too, Miss Adriano, but really, do you feel any of us should interfere with a decision of such magnitude? There will be other people involved, you know, on both levels."

"I don't care," returned Ida flatly, "I need him here. I want him here."

Ida sat, weighing matters, for some time after Rose had left the office. Dammit, it wasn't fair. The work was going so well. Why did the Group have to muck everything up just as the years of research and experimentation were beginning to produce predictive results? No. She would raise plenty of hell before they pulled it off.

On the other hand, she thought reluctantly, what if Bertram really wanted to go back to the M-level? Well, what did *he* know? By the time the Group finished their pressure tactics, any candidate would be thoroughly convinced of the moral and spiritual obligation to undertake it all. She'd seen it happen too many times. First, the shrinking, painful reluctance; then the thoughtful consideration; then the resignation; and in the end, the exultation of commitment to a contract. She could not remain silent while it happened to Bertram. If he went, it would be with her screeching ringing in his ears.

Still ... how much *did* the Group really and truly know which was beyond the knowledge of her level? She could not fully accept the prevailing concept of the infallibility of those unseen ones from a higher level. Nevertheless, there undoubtedly was, among them, reasoning of a higher quality, more direct communication with God (whatever or whoever He might finally turn out to be, and at this point, one guess was as good as another), and access to data which lay beyond her reach. Did she dare pit herself against such awesome beings?

Yes, by god!

And yet ... ?

PART THREE

"How do you know she can't lead a double life?"

—MAX MELCHIOR

Scott passed through the doorway, pausing to inspect the marble floor of the foyer. It was dusk and only a few hours remained before Eve would arrive. When she had last been here she had noted the lack of luster on its delicate rose surface and he had made a mental note to have it attended to before tonight. With satisfaction, he saw that the designer, Mr. Lantini, had conceived the authentic satin gleam, subtly reflecting the dark slender legs of the console table and the faceted chandelier. At either side of the doorless doorway, open to the panoramic view, stood urns of lilies, lush, head-high, faintly perfumed. He must thank the gardener for his ability to create them in such perfection.

Turning to face the view, he was as always humbled by its majesty. Below the house the grounds spread like velvet, studded by formal plantings and graceful walks passing half-hidden pools. Beyond, through the deer park, the river glided. What did Eve call it? Shenandoah? But it was named Jupiter. She would never use that alien name; now, no longer would he. Behind the river valley rose the forest, with vast stands of every tree she knew and loved. He recalled how he had asked the designer whether he could create hemlock, pine and fir, oak and elm, cypress, magnolia, dogwood and wild plum. Hanging vines and flowering carpet and jeweled rocks, with flashing birds and deer and wild horses white as foam . . . all this genius provided, the hidden paths as well, and the altar, moss-grown . . .

His life of spiritual harmony and balance had made it possible for him to have all this. Such beauty as he was able to create for himself he had imagized and brought to visible form. Those luxuries that were beyond his capacity to create had accumulated even so, since the contributions he had made out of his own talents had merited their repayment out of the talents of others.

In the foyer he flashed Robert, who came at once, his face eager and inquiring.

"Well, Scott," he said, "you were a long time at the Archives."

"Yes, and had the very devil of a time of it, too. Accomplished little if anything at all," replied Scott, removing his cape. "Any messages?"

"Major Melchior, wanting to know whether you would be free this evening. I said you were expecting Eve but not until quite late."

"Did he say what he wanted of my evening?"

"He said that Mr. Higgins had asked for an appointment with you."

"An appointment? Why would Joel need an appointment?" Scott turned down the corridor toward his bedroom. "Besides, I ought to spend some time with Harriet this evening. She's been left alone all day."

"Not entirely alone," responded Robert, hurrying his lame foot to keep up with Scott's stride. "I have seen her now and then throughout the day."

"Oh? Good of you, Robert. How do you think she's adjusting?"

"Well enough to join us at dinner," replied Robert. "See what you think of her attitude."

Alone in his room, Scott tossed his ruffled shirt upon the bed and entered his dressing room. Higgins. It was not to be a social call, then. In the bath, the water flowed gently through the pool and fell over mossy stones. For once, he was unaware of the beauty of their sight and sound. He hesitated before stepping into the pool. His eyes darkened. Slowly he picked up the communicator and asked for Major Melchior.

The child was toddling on fat little legs across the room as Scott entered. The rounded face below pale gold fluff was fiercely intent upon the chess set which lay tumbled in tantalizing availability upon the floor just out of his reach. He looked up, pleasure written vividly upon the baby features, as he sensed Scott's presence.

"I'm glad you're here," the nurse exclaimed, rising from the floor where she had been playing with the boy. "I need a few minutes on the comm to reach my house."

"Of course, Mrs. Jessup," Scott replied, lifting the

little boy up into his arms. "I'm taking him into the garden for a time, so don't hurry."

The baby crawled across the grass, slapping his hands down hard with every stroke. Eve's son. Scott watched him, seeing how his features resembled hers. He smiled, calling, "Matthew, come over here to me."

A pulse began to beat, hard, in his temple. In his mind he could see Eve as she was during the days just before her miscarriage. He felt depression descend— even something more than depression—embedding itself malignantly in his auric field. Gathering up the child, he flashed for Robert.

"Take Matthew until Mrs. Jessup returns," he told him hastily, depositing the baby in Robert's arms. "I must try again to reach Major Melchior."

"Very well," replied Robert, examining Scott closely. "And you will be pleased to know that Harriet has agreed to take late supper with us when Eve arrives."

Scarcely hearing, Scott left the garden, striding rapidly. In the dining room he saw the damask table laid, the tapers waiting. Not stopping to select the wine, as was his custom so that all should be in readiness before she came, he hurried on to their bedroom.

Again Max did not answer his flash.

He felt the foreboding deepen. He was without question registering some intelligence outside himself. Where the devil was Max at a time like this?

Robert's flash from downstairs interrupted his concentration.

"Scott," the voice said, "Mr. Higgins is here."

The two friends, seated in deep chairs in Scott's study, had fallen into an awkward silence after their attempts at opening civilities. Higgins was regarding him oddly, Scott thought. Could the imperturbable Higgins be wearing an expression of compassion?

"What is it, Joel?" he asked gently. "Come, old friend. Perhaps I can make your task easier. Have you come calling in your official capacity to offer me a contract for return to the mortal level? If so, I shall send my regrets to the Group. I have plans of my own." He tried to smile.

"My dear fellow," replied Higgins, with difficulty, "it is precisely those plans which bring me to you. It has come to my attention that those plans involve the deliberate ending of Eve's mortal embodiment before its course is run."

"Did your informant also reveal to you that our plan does not involve an overt act? That we consider it morally acceptable for Eve to simply relinquish her survival mechanisms?"

"A shabby rationalization, Scott," retorted Higgins. "One which changes nothing, in my opinion."

"On the contrary," Scott said. "It is a matter of the right to choose."

"One's choices sometimes take their toll of others," Higgins observed. "Do you proclaim the rights of two small children to their mother's ministry as vigorously as you proclaim your own and Eve's?"

"Yes," Scott answered. "I compute their rights along with the rights of her son on this plane and add our own right to be together. I do not espouse self-sacrifice for sacrifice's sake."

"You give me pause, Scott." Higgins fell silent under Scott's burning eyes.

"Have I surprised you with my views?" Scott asked.

"If so, no more, perhaps, than your ministerial role surprises me."

"Ah, Scott, and I surprise myself, as well," sighed Higgins. "In any case, I did not come in any priestly capacity. The subject of my visit is quite different."

"I know, Joel. I sensed your thoughts before you arrived. Do you face a difficult task, old chap? Have you come bearing ill-tidings?" Again Scott attempted to smile.

"Yes, to both questions," Higgins replied. He rose from his chair and began to examine the richly bound books which lay upon the library table. Scott did not speak, and when Higgins glanced quickly over his shoulder his heart contracted at the look upon Scott's face as he sat quietly, waiting.

"Scott," Higgins said, finally, "the question of the morality of your plan is moot. Whether it be justified or not, the fact is that it must not, cannot, be implemented. I have received information from the Higher Ones which absolutely precludes Eve's relinquishment of her survival mechanisms. My poor chap, I must tell you that Eve's commitment will hold her in the mortal plane for the natural course of her lifetime."

Still Scott did not speak, and Higgins continued haltingly. "The ultimate purpose of Project Jupiter, as you are aware, is to compile data on the effects of interplane communication, embracing contacts between our level and the mortal level, as well as between our level and the level of the Higher Ones; that is, to scrutinize the quality of present methods and to seek improvement, if possible. More than that, the goal is to determine to what extent communication is beneficial, or if, indeed, it is desirable at all. Eve is one of many who have agreed to take part in the Experiment, an experiment to determine what happens when people on separate levels interact in full knowledge of one another."

Scott was hearing Higgins' words with difficulty. Everything Joel was saying had been long familiar to Scott. He saw Higgins' earnest face through a moving blur.

"In God's name, Joel, come out with it!" he cried.

Higgins resumed his seat near Scott's chair and leaning close, grasped Scott's arm. "Eve is contracted to bring into mortal expression a child who is under commitment to the Jupiter Experiment." Fixing his eyes on Scott's, he added softly, "She must remain there. Must survive there."

A steady and increasing pressure enveloped Scott's body, bearing inward. The lamplight faded. He could no longer see Higgins' face.

"Joel ..." he said, whispering, but he could hear no reply....

Scott was climbing rapidly up the face of a steep cliff. His feet and legs were bare and the jutting stones cut painfully into his flesh. Presently he saw that the cliff's face was splattered with small black droplets, and looking above him to the place where a narrow ledge projected, he saw their source. Streaming over the rim of the ledge the black stain spread, and streaks lay slanted where the blood had run, spilling, dripping far below into the gorge. He had found her.

Frantic, he closed the space between them. Eve lay dead upon the bloody stone. Matthew lay beside her. No, it was not Matthew. The boy was older than Matthew. He lay with his frail limbs wrapped about her body, clinging.

Scott lifted her ... began to climb with her down the cliff.... The boy followed....

Higgins could not rouse Scott. After some moments had passed, he realized what had happened and no longer tried to wake him. Scott had been taken by the Source into an out-of-time experience. Higgins sat patiently and with respect, in the ancient prayer position, waiting.

Scott lifted his head at last and looked squarely into Higgins' eyes. "They have taken her again, Joel," he said.

"Who has taken her?" Higgins asked softly. "Who are 'they'?" he repeated.

"The old gods," answered Scott. "It was only the old gods, Joel. The Sun had nothing to do with it."

Making his departure, Higgins turned to Scott once more. "I beg you, Scott, let us discuss this again at a more propitious time," he urged. "Perhaps when you have had the time for prayer and meditation?"

Scott stood stiffly, his hands gripped one upon the other behind his back. "My answer would be the same," he said. "Tell the Group that I accept the first requirement, that Eve live out her mortal span. Tell them also that I reject the second, that she fulfill this task while continuing her life with me. Tell the Group that I give her up. That I give her up on my own terms, and utterly, while her mortal life shall last."

Higgins bowed his head. "Dear old fellow," he said, "I have pressed you past reason."

Alone in the corridor, Scott, moving slowly, blindly, turned toward the terrace. It was ending, and the last days were upon them. How many times could he bring Eve again to this house before they must part? The coming child, precious in any case but even more precious because of its special value to the Project, must come before all else. He knew he must not continue to overshadow Eve's life during the many years she would need to remain on the M-level, the impingement of their relationship upon her mortal life already having proved deleterious. She must live in one world at a time. She must no longer be torn. To fulfill her role as mother of this exceptional child, she must not be a fragmented personality. And he remembered how he had comforted her, saying that in the end, although separated for a time, they two—being joined by an Almighty Hand—could never be, would never be, completely apart.

Across the valley the mountains rose, eternal. Lifting his eyes, Scott spoke silently. "Fill me," he asked.

"I will fill you," was the answer.

He was aware of Matthew's cry coming from the nursery wing. The sound of the baby's voice penetrated his preoccupation. Ah, he thought, I am not alone in my bereavement. This helpless child, having no voice in this decision, trusts and is betrayed, never more while mortal life should last, to see his mother's face. He walked, quite steadily, in the direction of the nursery.

On the way he came face to face with Robert.

"I spoke," said Robert, anxiously. "Didn't you hear?"

Scott focused on Robert with great effort.

"Harriet is ready for her discussion hour. Do you want to go to her now?" Robert asked.

"Robert, dear friend," Scott said, haltingly. "There has been bad news. When Eve arrives she must be left with me in absolute seclusion. I count on you, as always."

"And Harriet?" persisted Robert.

"Get in touch with Major Melchior and say that you are returning Harriet to the hospital," he told Robert, woodenly. "I cannot help her now."

"Scott, please—"

Scott did not answer.

"Scott, let me try. I can take care of her."

Scott was already proceeding down the hall to Matthew's room. "Ask Max," he said absently, over his shoulder.

He opened the door and entered, stepping very slowly and carefully, closing the door softly behind him. The baby's wail changed soon to sounds of pleasure.

Soberly, Robert removed the formal table settings. He would arrange, for Scott and Eve, the small supper table in their bedroom. It would be illumined from nearby by the beautiful and elaborate candelabrum that had been Scott's gift to her when she had turned nineteen. But to them, Robert knew, it was symbolic of much more than the marking of a birthday. Whatever it was that Eve must face, perhaps it would be easier to approach beneath the living flames of the nineteen candles. Robert longed to help her, to comfort her, to speak to her of hope. But he would not intrude. Tonight they would dine alone.

"Scott, I've gone over this in detail with Joel," said Max. "Can't I persuade you to change your mind?"

They were seated in Max's office, the privacy screen glowing softly about the room.

"You must know how glad I would be to find justification for changing my mind," said Scott.

"I'm not offering you a rationalization. I'm trying to get it through your head what the Planning Group has to say about your situation."

"You've made it abundantly clear as to the viewpoint of the Planning Group," replied Scott, somewhat testily. "I have agreed to their first requirement. It is my refusal to accept the second requirement that troubles you."

"Let's take another look at it, Scott," urged Max. "The Group sees this from the standpoint of Project Jupiter, right? The progress of the Project supercedes concern for the individual. You're the one who explained that whole bit to me, a long time ago, remember? I don't have to tell you that when you and Eve volunteered for service you both knew it would involve experimenting with the effects of interplane communication. As they see it, if Eve is beginning to carry over to the M-level some memories of her real identity, so much the better."

"We volunteered our services to God," said Scott. "And we have accepted the commitments as they have been revealed, and at whatever costs. Even now we are honoring our pledge. I am only insisting that we do so in such a way as to spare Eve unnecessary suffering."

"You call it sparing her, putting a stop to her night travel, to her life here with you and Matthew, with all of us? I don't get it. How big-hearted can you get?"

"Max, think. Eve will have many years to live on the

M before she will be free, her tasks finished. I want her to do it as comfortably as possible, without being haunted by our life together."

"Oh, fine," said Max, in exasperation. "Fine and dandy. You are generous enough to let her have this baby and live out the incarnation without you, cut off from the real, from her home base here on the IM. And all so that she can be 'comfortable'? What the hell kind of logic is that?"

"I realize how difficult it will be, but you see, the alternative is unthinkable."

"You mean, for her to end the M-life and cop out on the whole scene? You're right, that is unthinkable," agreed Max.

"No, I didn't mean that, because Eve would never consider that as an alternative—not now."

"Why not? You mean on account of the new baby? You said she was all set to leave the two she already has."

"It was not an easy decision to make, Max."

"No, it was tough, but she made it, didn't she?"

"We were not offered the luxury of an ideal solution. Once Eve began to remember me during her mortal hours, her life with Warner and the children was impinged upon. She cannot lead a double life. A choice had to be made."

"How do you know she can't lead a double life? You won't give her a chance to work it out."

"Max, Eve's principles would never permit her to knowingly be involved with two men at the same time. She and I have been together through many of these incarnations, and I know her. I know her on the basic level."

"Oh ho!" said Max. "Now we just may be getting somewhere. Out of all those incarnations you found out about at the Archives, the only one you really remember is the last one, and the Victorian barnacles from that one are still thick on you. *That's* where all this monogamy is coming from! You're not making this decision from the basic level, my friend."

"Eve was with me in that life and has as many Victorian scruples as I have."

"You don't know that, Scott. After all, Eve has reincarnated and you haven't. She's no longer simply the woman you knew and loved on your last trip. She's picked up a genetic line, had a twentieth-century background, experiences, education, that she didn't have in that other lifetime. You can't say what capabilities she has now."

"Nevertheless, her capabilities do not include proceeding with life in two worlds."

"So, while you could justify her leaving her two children through death—say through attracting some kind of illness or accident—in order to 'make a choice,' you can't justify her leaving the child that's on the way now. Okay, I understand that. Her compact with the Group says she is indispensible to this baby. So what is the alternative that's so unthinkable?"

"Why, Max, it is a lifetime of divided loyalty, of guilt, of all that goes with a double involvement. A sense of incompleteness, no matter which family she's with. My shadow falling across her happiness with Warner."

"Look, Scott," said Max, out of patience. "I'm going to tell you what you're doing. You're acting as if you and Eve and Matthew would be living on Maple Street in Boston in a house, and across town she'd be living in another house with Warner and the two kids, and she'd be hot-footing it back and forth between the two."

"An ugly picture."

"Yeah, especially the part about her going from your bed to Warner's, right? Isn't that what it boils down to, old buddy? Isn't that what you think Eve can't stand knowing about?"

"Of course it is," answered Scott.

"But it was perfectly all right as long as she didn't know she was doing it, huh?"

"You are beginning to offend me, Max."

"I know it, but for God's sake, you've got to get the right attitude, somehow. I can't help it if you take a burn."

"I think my attitude is understandable—to a man of honor."

"Who said it wasn't? But it's not the attitude that's going to work toward the highest good."

"If you mean," said Scott, "that it's not the attitude the Planning Group would like me to entertain, I agree."

"When I first came to this level, my friend, and you took me under your wing, ruffled shirt and all, what did you tell me about attitude? 'Attitude is all,' you said. It's the way you look at things that matters, not things themselves. And you said that usually you can make a conscious decision as to what attitude to take."

"True," said Scott. "And I have made my decision."

Max jumped up from his chair. "Of all the pious ...! Who do you think you are, setting yourself up to decide on the rest of Eve's incarnation?" he shouted.

"I am fulfilling a role with which you are unfamiliar,

judging from your treatment of Ida," retorted Scott. "I am protecting my Beloved as best I can."

"Oy gevalt," moaned Max. "Look, you're a hundred years behind the times, literally. Who the hell asked you for protection? Did Eve? You're damn right she didn't! Why can't you let *her* decide what she can handle? Is she a person, Scott? Is she? Or an appendage of yours?"

Scott was on his feet, but before he could make his heated reply, Ida entered the office, looking pretty in a simple blue dress and appearing much too innocent.

"Hi, guys," said she, carefully casual. "Did I hear my name mentioned?"

"Didn't you see the privacy screen?" demanded Max, indignantly.

"Sure, I saw it, lover," she said, sprawling in a chair lazily. "It's just that I have a rotten attitude toward your privacy."

Max and Scott were staring grimly at each other.

"I just ordered champagne sent up," she ventured helpfully.

"Champagne won't help, Ida," growled Max.

"I know," she said, "but it's time for a breather."

M-level

The two girls sat on the couch, comfortably dressed in robes, as they had done so many times before during their long friendship. Eve's face was strained and she kept tossing her long hair over her shoulders as though it burdened her. Mary Kay went into the kitchen and came back with the coffee maker, setting it on the low table. Looks like it's going to be a long night, she thought.

Settling herself again on the couch, she said carefully, "Listen, I just don't get it, Evie. You have a terrific life from where I sit. I don't see the problem, not at all."

"Well, you see," replied Eve, her fingers worrying the fringe on a cushion, "the problem is the guilt. That's perfectly simple."

Mary Kay smothered a momentary feeling of irritation. Eve's life, it seemed to her, was the picture-book ideal. What did Eve know of financial stress, or of a driving need to accomplish something, just one thing, outside the family framework, or of a husband who was consistently destructive of her self-esteem? Eve had everything; had gotten it easily, in exchange for her inborn beauty, sensitivity and intelligence, and her air of mystery.

"What simple?" she said testily. "Aren't you dramatizing this thing? I don't understand. Guilt? About what?"

Eve looked at Mary Kay with clear and innocent eyes. "Why, I'm guilty of wanting to die," she said.

Mary Kay was filled with a thrilling urge to slap Eve soundly across that dreaming face, to snatch her back from some far place by pain and shock and fury.

"For the love of God, Eve," she said, spilling her coffee as she set down the cup, "what's the matter with you?"

"Well," said Eve quietly, "I think the trouble is probably that something is wrong with my mind. I need to talk to Max."

And now they sat at the table with the board as they had done so many times before in Chicago. Eve had never seen Mary Kay work alone. She herself had been completely unsuccessful in the several attempts she had made to operate alone, and now, the warm greetings over, she expressed to Max her yearning to be able to contact him without help.

"I am having trouble, Max," she told him, "and I needed to talk to you, but there was no way. Don't I have any psychic ability at all?"

"That's what I have to tell you about, Eve," Max replied. The planchette was moving slowly and heavily under Mary Kay's fingertips. She shifted uncomfortably in her chair.

"I know about what's been going on in your mind, Evie," he continued, "and the only solution is for me to explain some things to you."

Dear Max, thought Eve. She felt comforted already.

"Evie," he proceeded, "you've been thinking of ending your life, but you don't know why."

"That's just it," exclaimed Eve, "there *is* no reason. That's why I am so ashamed. I don't want to leave Warner and the children. I miss them all, right now. So how could I bear—" she broke off, her voice a little tearful. "I don't really want to die," she continued painfully after a moment. "People who think about suicide want to get away from something hard. Or hurt someone. Or get attention, you know, even if it kills them." She gave a shaky little laugh. "But I'm okay. I have no problems."

"None of these are your problem," replied Max. "With you, it's not wanting to escape something; it's wanting to go to something."

"To something?"

"To someone."

"To someone?" echoed Eve. "But if I kill myself— Or rather, if I let myself die, say by getting sick, or drowning in the pool, or something—then how could I go ..." Puzzled, she said nothing more. The planchette moved in circles. Max was waiting.

"You mean, to someone in *your* world," she said at last. "But that's impossible. There's no one in that world that I'm even close to except you, and you're not ... well, you know, I wouldn't ..."

"Listen, Eve," said Max, "what you wanted to find out from me was what happens to you on my side if you take your life, and that's what I'm telling you."

"No, you aren't," she protested, "You're telling me I want to be with someone over there."

"This world is not really *over* anywhere or *up* anywhere, but that's another subject. I'm trying to tell you what it will be like if you do it. See, it depends on your motive, to a large extent, what happens to you."

"Never mind that," Eve said distractedly. "I've heard that if you commit suicide you are earthbound forever. Like you were, at first. Is that how it is?"

"Earthbound is another subject, too," he answered, "and that depends, also. But if you want to know, if you do go ahead and do it, deliberately or semi-deliberately, you will end up in my hospital, for therapy."

"Therapy? What kind of therapy?"

"Well," said Max, "that's another thing that depends. Like, how do you intend to do it? With a gun? That would be a violent—"

Mary Kay took her hands from the planchette and

began to massage the back of her neck where the pain was spreading.

"I'm not going any further with this, Max Melchior," she said tightly.

"What's the matter?" asked Eve, fully aware of Mary Kay for the first time in several minutes.

"I don't like his attitude," retorted Mary Kay.

"Max's attitude? But I'm the one who is upset, not Max."

"Well, then I don't like it that he is discussing this at all. And as casually as planning to bake a cake!"

"But I asked him. I want to know what it's like," said Eve, "because what if I should do it? It's getting like a compulsion. I can't brush it off. It's a growing desire to be over and out, that's all—and soon! No reasons. That's why I'm taking this seriously—with a compulsion you don't need a reason, you do it whether you want to or not, whether you should or not. So what if—"

"Oh, you're not going to kill yourself, for heaven's sake!" cried Mary Kay irritably. "How silly can we get? This is just ridiculous! You and Max shouldn't be talking about this at all. The whole thing is crazy. I won't go on with it." She jumped up from the table and poured a cup of coffee with a shaking hand.

"But Mary Kay," Eve said earnestly, "don't you see? If it *should* happen, I wouldn't know what to expect. Please let Max—"

"You don't need to know."

"I must know."

Something in her tone made Mary Kay look at Eve sharply. Slowly, without a word, she took her seat at the board again.

"When physical death is violent—and to some extent even if it's *not* violent but just sudden—there is considerable shock, and that causes a confused mental state. We have methods now that help shorten the duration of this. That's the kind of therapy I meant you would need. Some people need emotional therapy depending on the hangup that made them do it."

"But I don't have any motive at all," Eve protested, "in fact, it's the very opposite—I'm motivated *not* to do it."

"No," said Max, "you want to."

"Max, are you out of your mind, for the love of God?" cried Mary Kay, pushing back her chair.

"Stop—" said Max just before she took her hands from the planchette. In spite of herself, Mary Kay resumed her position at the board. "Stop jumping up like that, sweetie," he told her, "I know what I'm doing."

"Like hell you do," Mary Kay shot back. "You're talking Eve into it, and I'm being made a party to it."

"Max," Eve asked, "why do I want to die?"

"You want to be with someone you love."

"No."

"Suit yourself," replied Max. The planchette circled.

"Whom do I want to be with badly enough to do such a thing?" Eve asked at last.

"Ha," returned Max, "I thought you'd never ask. And grammatically, too."

"You see," said Mary Kay, "you see what I mean? Jokes, yet."

"That hurts, Mary Kay," Max said, circling dejectedly.

"Oh, all right," Mary Kay sighed. "Who is it, then?"

"It's a long story how you came to feel this deeply about this person, and you wouldn't believe me anyhow, Eve. The reason I have to explain the best I can is that you need to know what has been wrong with you. You've had a conflict going between your love for Warner and for this man I'm speaking of."

The planchette stopped. Mary Kay could not go on. Eve, speechless, was staring at her. They sat in silence. Finally Mary Kay took Eve's hand across the table.

"Evie," she asked gently, "what do you want me to do? Do you want me to go on?"

Eve nodded, not looking up.

Neither of them spoke.

"I'm sorry," Max said, "but I had to tell you."

"Oh, Max, it's all right, I'm not upset," Eve said quietly. "You see, I don't believe a word of it."

"I know," he said, "so I guess we might as well drop the subject for now. But let me just say this: the candlelight is light enough."

IM-level

The girls still sat at the table, worn out by the emotional discussion that had followed the lengthy sitting. Their unseen friends stood about them, regarding them appraisingly. Max leaned over and kissed the back of Mary Kay's neck.

"It's times like this I wish they could see us," he said to the others, "especially Mary. Did you see how she stuck by me all the way?"

"An accomplished operator," agreed Joel Higgins

smiling. "I thought the entire job went rather well, actually."

"Well," said Ida from where she stood, her hands on Eve's shoulders, "I don't know about that, Joel. It was a lot to hand her all at once. You almost lost contact, Max, with your flippant attitude."

"Oh, come on, baby," said Max, "you know that's the way I work. Mary gets fuzzy if the mood gets heavy."

"I don't care," Ida retorted, "you'll be lucky if Mary doesn't quit for good after tonight."

Max looked down at Mary Kay's drawn face, her tousled hair. Patting her cheek, he smiled. "No," he said, "Mary won't quit."

Projecting back to Max's living room, the three made themselves comfortable. Ida, in her soft rose-colored gown, curled up in the deep satin chair.

"Max, how about a bottle of champagne?" she suggested, "and something to eat, too, come to think of it. I seem to have run out of gas."

Max left the room, pulling off his blue sweater as he went. Higgins seated himself on the low sofa and turned to Ida.

"Perhaps this is an opportune time for me to have a discussion with you on a rather urgent matter," he began.

Ida felt the warning signal in her aura light. "Not tonight, Joel," she said lightly. "I told you, I'm tired."

Higgins sat up, erect. "We cannot continue to postpone this, Ida."

"Maybe *you* can't," she said, throwing her legs over the arm of her chair in her favorite posture. "I can put it off if I want to." She stretched luxuriously. "Where is Max with that champagne?"

"I must submit a report on Bertram without further delay," persisted Higgins.

"Will you for God's sake leave me alone about Bertram?" cried Ida, "I can't take any more psychic burn right now."

"You are aware that timing is vital in these matters. The Planning Group says—"

"Screw the Planning Group!" returned Ida. "What do they care about my department, or poor Bertram, either?"

Higgins stared at her in stunned silence.

Max entered carrying a tray on which were an ice bucket with a champagne bottle, three glasses and a plate of thin sandwiches. He lowered the tray to the table, and pouring a glass, offered it to Ida. She accepted it without comment and drained it.

"Champagne, Joel?" Max held out his glass.

"Thank you, no," said Higgins, disapprovingly.

"What's going on in here?" asked Max, eyeing Ida's stormy face.

"Joel is badgering me to make up my mind about Bertram," Ida told him.

"Oh," said Max, "no wonder. You know how Ida depends on Bertram. She plans to try to stop you and your plan for him."

"I must remind you that it is not *my* plan but the desire of the Group. I must know to what extent she has decided to oppose my efforts to facilitate the plan."

"Well, this isn't the time, Joel, and besides, we're expecting Scott any minute, you know."

"Very well, then," said Higgins, resigned for the time being. "I shall flash you tomorrow at your office, Ida."

Ida sipped her second glass of champagne moodily. No one spoke. They waited silently for Scott.

Ida met Scott at the door. When she saw his face she put her arms about him impulsively. Neither of them could speak. Together they passed into the living room where Max and Higgins waited.

"Well, Scott," said Max, gripping his hand, "I did the best I could, that's all I can say."

"I know," Scott replied, taking the chair Max offered, "but it still seems to me I should have been with her when you told her."

"Scott, we agreed before I went that I couldn't handle it with you there," reminded Max gently.

Scott said nothing.

"Look, Scott," Ida intervened, "Max is too close to you and Eve. He's emotionally involved." She pushed her hair back from her face distractedly. "Me, too," she added.

"Eve will make her adjustment smoothly enough, Scott," put in Higgins, sympathetically.

Scott lifted his hands slightly and let them fall to his knees. "I knew before you went that it would be difficult for all concerned. I thank you, truly thank you. It's simply that it was even more painful for her than I had believed it would be ..."

"I can see how she feels," said Ida. "She didn't want to believe it. She can't conceive of loving two men at the same time, even if they are in different worlds, and if you want the truth, neither can I."

"That was my meaning when I said she would adjust," said Higgins. "As time passes, she will learn to keep the two worlds separated."

"Oh, how do you know, Joel," Ida said impatiently. "You are forever making statements as fact. That's just an opinion."

"On the contrary," replied Higgins firmly, "the Planning Group has long since established that in these cases of separated mates, the incarnate partner accommodates..."

"There he goes again with that eternal Planning Group," she said to Max, casting her eyes to the ceiling. "I get tired of hearing about them. They've all been Upstairs so long they've gotten out of touch with what it's really like on our level, let alone on the M-level."

"I really must protest," said Higgins. "To speak of the Group as you do amounts to blasphemy."

"What!" cried Ida, incensed. "They aren't God! They're nothing but spirits!"

"—devoted to our welfare, in the eternal sense," reminded Higgins.

"Yes, and a fine mess they make, too! Lots of times! Look at Eve, Joel. As soon as she accepts Scott, she's going to start asking what about Warner."

"Ida," warned Max, glancing at Scott, who was listening gravely.

"You mean don't mention Warner in front of Scott, for God's sake, as if Scott's no more than a jealous lover?"

"That's enough, Ida."

"The hell it is," she gritted. "I'm just getting started."

"Not now," Max ordered.

"It's all right, Ida," Scott intervened. "Your questions are legitimate. I, too, would like the answers. They are part of our dilemma."

"It's just that I think Eve is in such a rotten spot,"

Ida said, somewhat mollified. "You know, because when she's on the M-level she doesn't know about everything here, and now that you've told her about Scott, right away she's going to start feeling unfaithful."

"Yes, indeed," Scott said, "but to whom?"

"I see," said Ida, "you've thought of all these complications yourself."

"Precisely."

"Scott," she asked, "let me ask you the big one. Have you wondered what happens to Warner when he arrives on our level and finds you and Eve committed to one another?"

"Ida," said Max, obviously annoyed, "I wish you would stop acting as if you had no briefing on this case at all. You knew all about it before we went to Eve tonight. Why did you wait until now to bring all this up?"

"Because you all said Eve had to be prevented from suicide, and that was uppermost in my mind. I guess I thought we were just going to explain that there was nothing wrong with her, that it was only that she was starting to tune in on this spirit lover, so stop worrying, Eve, and don't kill yourself because you can't because you're going to have a baby ... you know, just the bare bones of the situation, just enough to make her straighten out and fly right. I didn't realize, quite, how it would sound to her. And how she would feel about it. And then the news about the baby. I think it was just too much for her in such a short time."

"We had to tell her all of it while we had the chance," replied Max. "We couldn't risk anything happening to the child."

"Well, anyway, she won't kill herself," Ida said. "She didn't believe it. Toward the end, not any of it."

"She will come to believe it," said Scott quietly. "Her perception is increasing steadily. If she remembers me, she will try to come to me."

Standing to leave, Higgins turned to Scott. "No, my friend, she will not come to you. When she realizes that the message about the child is true, she will honor her contract."

"Yes," said Scott. "You are right, Joel. I know you are right."

Higgins could no longer look at Scott's face. "Well, goodnight, then," he said awkwardly. "Ida, I will speak with you tomorrow."

When he was gone they sat wrapped in thought. Scott and Max appeared to be in reverie, Ida noticed. We're waiting for Eve to fall asleep, Max answered her silent question.

Ida dozed, and when she opened her eyes again, Scott was gone. Max was looking at her through half-closed eyelids.

"You know what?" she asked drowsily. "Nobody answered my question."

"What question?"

"The one about what happens to Warner."

"Well, don't ask me," he yawned, "I just work here."

M-level

Mary Kay turned on the bedside lamp and sat up in bed. There was no sound from the sun parlor that doubled as guest room. Was Eve sleeping? Mary Kay sensed that she was not. Impulsively she started to the door. She would go to Eve. Hesitating at the doorway, she changed her mind. They had talked for hours yet neither of them was reassured. More talk would not help. It was very late. If only she could get a little sleep before the long day with the children began! They would need to talk to Max again, of course, and it would be difficult if she were tired. Plumping her pillows and smoothing the sheets, she tried once more to compose herself for sleep, but she could not.

She was still angry, that was the trouble. Fervently she wished that she could discard the entire night's work as foolish fantasy. In fact, did she really believe it? She did not know. If it were not true, then of course it was coming from some level of her own mind. This excellent possibility was almost as disturbing as its alternative. That was the trouble with doing psychic work in the first place, she thought rebelliously—it had to be explained. She would stop it, she told herself. It had been such a source of pleasure in the beginning, but now so often it was disturbing. And tonight—tonight for the first time she faced the possibility that her psychic work could do real harm to someone.

But Eve had been considering suicide! Whatever its source, at least the night's work appeared to have averted that.

Even so, Mary Kay reasoned, she was not qualified to interfere. If Eve was actually suicidal, then Warner should know of it and Eve should be receiving competent professional care.

Heartsick, Mary Kay flung herself across the bed. Her head throbbed and there was the familiar deep pain in her lower back. She was filled with a sensation of distaste.

Eve drew her negligee around her and leaned forward in the window seat. The sheer curtains, drawn back, were like mist in the dark room. Outside, the outlines of Mary Kay's garden showed faintly in the starlight. Soon dawn would come and all would seem normal again. There was nothing to worry about. Max's story could not be true.

Eyes closed, she sat quietly, waiting for the dawn. A deep sadness welled in her, strange and final.

"But it *is* true," she whispered.

She slept, her head against the casement, her loose robe falling about her.

Scott lifted her then, and took her home.

Eve was dressing for the plane trip home. Mary Kay sat watching, silent. After three days of talk, there was no more to be said. Eve, though a trifle pale, appeared serene enough. It was Mary Kay who was nearing tears, for the first time during the past days. She felt emotionally drained, both from the psychic work and from emotion, and the low backache which often resulted from psychic effort had become intense.

Ready to leave now, Eve turned to Mary Kay. "Could we just say goodbye to Max?" she asked, tentatively.

"We said goodbye last night," answered Mary Kay sullenly.

"Just for a minute," urged Eve. "I won't open it all up again."

At the board, waiting for Max, Eve looked at Mary Kay's grim face. "Don't feel that way. Please don't feel that way."

"I can't help it."

Now Max was ready. "Greetings, earthlings," he wrote breezily.

"Max," said Eve, "darling Max. Thank you for what you tried to do."

"You bet," said Max. "Love and kisses." It was his familiar sign-off. Mary Kay could no longer restrain her tears.

It was time to leave for the downtown hotel, to join Warner for the trip home.

Mary Kay passed through the days of waiting for Kenneth to return as if in a long and painful dream. Chrissy developed an ear infection and Mary Kay took him to the pediatrician and cared for him conscientiously but absentmindedly. The second-hand washing machine refused to spin and she wrung clothes by hand, hanging them indifferently here and there about the small house to dry. Nausea began to plague her, particularly in the mornings, as her entire body upon her awakening, rebelled against beginning another day.

It occurred to her that she might be pregnant, and she smiled sardonically at the thought. In his big Annunciation scene, had Max slipped up on the cast? Even worse, had she herself made an error in perception? Max had always said that in her work she made the perception psychically, her pickups then being manifested, involuntarily, through her own physical mechanism, upon the board. So if there was error, she knew, it was likely to be her own.

Further, there were possibilities beyond simple errors in perception. In picking up Max's verbalization of a thought that she had received in a block, there was always the danger that she might alter or embellish, in order to give expression to her own conscious or subconscious desires and tastes. But the implications of the material she had produced for Eve over the three-day period had so disturbed and revolted her that it was difficult for her to accept the idea that she could have fabricated, subliminally, any part of such a tale. Most unpalatable of all was Max's assertion that Eve was to bear a child (oh, naturally, a special child!—it fit the script) and for that reason must forego the self-indulgence of a suicide that would enable her to join a spirit lover who (again, naturally!) sounded like Robert Browning. The whole outrageously corny story, she fumed, was so offensive to her that she was comforted by that very fact—for there was no way, no way at all, that she could have originated this material because her own subconscious mind would have rebelled as strongly as did her conscious mind.

But what if there was a way? What would a psychologist say about it? The same thing she herself would say, she thought wryly, if this had happened to two other girls. That in some deep level of her unconscious, Mary Kay envied Eve—Eve, who had everything Mary Kay didn't have, especially Warner, the ideal lover-husband. That in presenting Eve with this Spirit Lover deal, Mary Kay was fulfilling her own unsatisfied needs, vicariously. That she was relishing the drama and romance of the situation, while at the same time righteously preserving her own purity of conscience, thereby feeling superior to Eve, poor Eve, who must struggle with a complicated knot of loyalties.

Worse yet, Mary Kay gasped inwardly, was the possibility that Mary Kay, in foisting this proposition on Eve, would strike a blow to Eve's marriage, an eventuality from which Mary Kay might derive a hidden satisfaction. Oh, God! groaned Mary Kay.

Faced with these possibilities, Mary Kay was overwhelmed with a sense of degradation and grief. The sincerity of her precious friendship with Eve, her confidence in her own moral character, the integrity of her psychic work—all were now open to question.

By the time Kenneth arrived home Mary Kay was physically ill. She met him at the door in her old bathrobe and fell into his arms, almost crying with the relief and joy of having him home.

Later, the hastily contrived dinner over and the children in bed, Mary Kay curled up on the sofa beside him and told him the whole story of Eve's visit, including a slightly censored account of her reaction to it.

"I don't see what you're so upset about," said Kenneth, in the patronizing tone that always infuriated Mary Kay. "You're taking it too seriously."

"Too seriously!" cried Mary Kay in disbelief. "Don't you understand at all? After all these years of work and study, after all I've heard about the pitfalls of psychic work, after all I thought I'd learned to avoid—and now it's happened to *me*! And Eve, of all people, is the one who is going to get hurt by it."

"Hurt, hell," responded Kenneth. "If Eve wants to let

this get to her then it's her responsibility, not yours. Why are you trying to figure out a way to take the blame?"

"Because I ... well, because I brought it all through on my board."

"And so what's the problem?"

"What's the problem? What's the problem? Just that now I've got Eve saddled up with a Spirit Lover, that's all! Never mind if it's true she's pregnant, as Max claims she is. You want a problem, I'll give you a problem. What about Warner? What about her marriage? Don't you see?"

"I see the thing I've always warned you about," said Kenneth irritably, "and that is that you're taking too seriously the material that you get. You're believing it."

"But Eve—"

"Eve, too. If a grown woman is stupid enough to take as gospel truth a mess of romantic garbage coming across on somebody's Ouija board, then I say it's her own funeral."

"You never told me before that you considered my work garbage," said Mary Kay, deeply hurt. "Who has kept egging me on all these years? What big-shot scientific genius has been threatening to spend money designing some big-shot instrument to further my work, my *garbage*?" Mary Kay's voice was shaking. "When all the time I need the money for a new washing machine," she added venomously.

"Well, you never got yourself in trouble before. You just talked to Max about life on his side, and things like that."

"Oh!" Mary Kay was incensed. "Be fair, Ken. That's not all I've done with my work and you know it! What about my Teacher? What about all I've learned from him?"

"Oh, well, he's okay. I mean—he just rambles on about love, and consciousness, and that kind of thing. He's never caused any trouble."

Mary Kay sprang to her feet. "I'm not going to sit here and listen while you patronize my Teacher!"

"Who's patronizing? I'm giving that guy plenty of credit. Really. He has a lot of good ideas. I mean that. He's done you a lot of good."

"Done *me* a lot of good? It's you he's been trying to enlighten. And anyway, why do you say that?"

"Well, because I *do* think he's helped you."

"How?" she asked, in spite of herself.

"Well, for one thing, he's kept your mind occupied—"

Mary Kay wheeled around toward him. "What a lousy thing to say! Is that what you call it? All my struggle for spiritual development? And just when I thought I was getting somewhere, now this! Look what's happened to me! And all you can see is that I was keeping my mind occupied!"

"So, *what's* happened to you? I'll tell you what's happened, Mary Kay. A mature woman invited herself to our home and asked you to produce psychic work for her. It was her idea, not yours. So you obliged. And you brought through a soap opera about a poetic lover over there but she must stay here on this side of the veil, roughing it with good old Warner, because she's pregnant. That's all that's happened to you. Big deal!"

"That's not the way it is at all. Don't you have the slightest bit of compassion for Eve? She didn't ask for *this*. Kenneth, it could ruin her relationship with Warner. Her whole life. And it's my fault—"

"Honey, will you listen to me? The only thing that's happened is that you two girls got together again and had some kicks working the Ouija board like you used to do. There's no evidence that there's any supernatural explanation for any material you ever received, then or now. All we know is that with the use of the board you are able to write material that you don't compose consciously. It's an interesting enough phenomenon for that reason alone. The stuff you get is coming from some source, but not necessarily from spirits. Can't you see that?"

"Oh, Ken, stop acting as if I were an idiot! You're not the only one who took psychology courses in school. And what do you think I've been doing, plowing through all those *ASPR Journals* all these years—reading Mother Goose stories? I know all the explanations for this kind of thing better than you do. I'm not so dumb that I don't know that ESP could have produced everything I've ever brought through. That poem that shook Eve up so—I know it's possible my own mind could have picked that up clairvoyantly. Even from a slip of paper 3000 miles away in California, where Eve had stuck it in her desk drawer and forgotten it. And for that matter, even though Eve hadn't mentioned it to me, or even thought about it since the day she wrote it, I know that it was available to me in her memory, nonetheless. All my sub had to do was to pick it up telepathically and make a big thing out of it. Anybody knows that—even your idiot wife. I just wish I could do it when I want to. I can think of ways I could make a fortune if I could figure out how to do it on demand. I could go to work for the Navy, make twice as much as you do, buy a washing machine. Or work for the CIA. They would flip over me—"

"Now, hon, calm down. I never said—"

"Anyway, in this case, the damage is already done. Eve didn't go into all that about proof. She wasn't interested in it. She just seemed to know. At first she tried not to believe it, because she didn't want to, but after the first jolt was over, she never questioned it. She just knew, like I know I'm me and you're you and we're sitting here yelling at one another. I tried to tell her. Offered to lend her books and stuff on how they think the paranormal works. But she said, oh what did they know about Max and them . . ."

"Well, if you realize all that, then why are you sick over it?" asked Kenneth, reasonably.

"Because in spite of it, Eve believes it. That's why."

"So okay, Eve believes it. But that's not all that bothers you, right? The real trouble is that you believe it, too."

"If you want the truth, yes, I believe it, and no, I don't have any reason to. That is exactly why I am so upset. And now, because of me, Eve's endangered. And another thing, it's a reflection on my work. It's a truism in psychic work that like attracts like. I've always had a high quality of content, you know, up till now. Wherever it originates, that makes me responsible."

"What are you talking about?"

"If it's from my sub, then what a rotten thing for me to dream up for poor Eve! On the other hand, if it's true—what Max says—then Max and his entire bunch are undeveloped, earthbound spirits and *I've* attracted them. So what does that make me?"

"Some kind of nut who thinks she's too developed to associate with Max!" retorted Kenneth. "Why is it you're not that choosy about friends on this side of the veil? Look at some of the people you pal around with—"

"Leave my friends out of this!" cried Mary Kay, "and by the way, why do you have to keep using that cultish expression, *the veil?*"

"I like it. It has a nice corny ring. Come on, hon, how come all your earthly friends aren't Masters and Teachers?"

"How come you're sticking up for Max when you don't even believe in him? You think it's my sub, remember?"

"There's no more proof that it's your sub than there's proof it's spirits. I'm saying we don't know where it originates, so why are you making yourself sick over it?"

"Well, don't worry. I won't let it happen again. I'm through with the whole thing. Absolutely through. Through. Through. Through. So let's stop talking about it, it's bringing on my nausea again."

"What nausea? You didn't tell me you were nauseated. See what I mean? You've got yourself all worked up."

"How do you know I'm not pregnant?"

"Pregnant? You mean you think you are?"

"Oh, no," she said smugly, "I have no proof, you know, so how could I possibly tell?"

"You knew with the others."

She looked at him silently. As Eve knows, she thought.

"Well, hon, maybe that's what you need. Something to take your mind off things, keep you busy."

In bed, Mary Kay turned her back to him. His apparent unawareness of her feelings filled her with resentment. When he flung his arm across her waist in his familiar gesture of affection, she lay coldly quiet.

"Now you don't have to design that fancy new board you wrote me about," she could not help saying, over her shoulder.

"I began the sketches on the plane coming home," he said. "I'm going to start on it right away."

"What for?" she asked bitterly. "I'm never going to touch that damn board again."

"Oh, you will," he assured her comfortably. "You've hit a good point for research. Of course you'll need a better board, though." Taking her in his arms he asked, "Still mad at me?"

Mary Kay sighed. "Ken, you just don't know me at all, do you?"

"Well, stranger," Kenneth chuckled, "what say you and I get acquainted?"

During the following weeks Mary Kay had three brief but affectionate notes from Eve, mentioning their experience with Max either not at all or in the most superficial way. Mary Kay answered them in kind, aware that they both were waiting.

Over her objections, Kenneth, true to his word, had begun work—and the expenditure of more money than they could afford—on the first model of his communication aid. That he would proceed in spite of her insistence that she was finished with "all that" infuriated

Mary Kay. His brushing aside of her feelings, his minimizing of what to her was a serious problem, and most of all his blithe assumption that she would "cooperate" as soon as the instrument was ready for testing, intensified her determination to never again resume her psychic work. In this dogged and rebellious mood, she answered the kitchen telephone one afternoon to hear Eve's voice speaking by long-distance from California.

"Mary Kay, it's definite," said Eve, without preamble. "Max was right. I'm pregnant."

Mary Kay could think of nothing to say which seemed appropriate. "How do you feel?" she asked finally, for want of a better response.

"I'm okay physically," replied Eve. "The trouble is, I've been writing more poems. Only I no longer think I'm writing them. I think I'm getting them psychically."

"But why is that a problem?" Mary Kay felt her hand on the telephone tighten. "I've always said you were sensitive," she said, carefully.

"It's not how I'm getting them that bothers me. It's what they say. As if they're messages . . ."

"So okay, they're messages."

"Oh, but Mary Kay, if they are . . . here's one, listen to this, it's not very long:

I saw a small gold bird upon a sumac hedge.
It brought tears to my throat, for its small defenseless head
Hung wearily. It did not sing, poor bird.

It was my bird—my very soul—so well beloved, so cherished,
And so I spoke, "Ah, little bird,

131

Ah, thou who slept within my hand only this morning
Thous dost not choose the hedge?
Thou'rt lost. In freedom sitting, still
Thou art not free, but lost.
Thy heart beats weakly save it beat against my palm."

I stretched my hand,
And with a small and wounded twittering
  —so sweet, so very gold and beautiful—
It found its way.

I lifted my eyes above the sumac hedge
And saw the rolling mountains green with pine,
And smelled the ferns, and heard the purling water,
And felt the expansion of my aura
  and that brave heart against my palm.

With a sense of sick finality, Mary Kay heard the strange and disembodied words coming through the receiver.

"Listen, Evie," she said desperately, "if you're saying that's Scott calling out to you from the Beyond, you can forget it! There isn't any Scott! None of it is true! It's all just something we made up, you and I, somehow, over the years, and this time we carried it too far. We went through all this, hour after hour, while you were here, remember? Let's not start it again. It isn't Scott you're picking it up from. Because there isn't any Scott. Except maybe as a storybook character we've dreamed up in our imaginations." She summed it up brutally, "If you're getting poems they are simply from some level of your own mind. So scratch 'Scott,' and cheer up. If you don't, next step is a head doctor."

"There *is* a Scott," Eve replied calmly. "I know the truth now. Only I don't know enough, that's all that's wrong. I need to talk to Scott himself. Hear from him, I mean."

"Oh, Eve, please, let's not stir it up again. I just can't. You know how I feel about it, I know you do."

"Of course I know and I don't blame you. But if you only knew what it's like, knowing just part of it. Maybe if I sent you the other poems he gave me . . . ?"

"There's not a poem in the world that would induce me to keep this thing alive in your heart," said Mary Kay earnestly. "Oh, Evie, can't you just be happy, like you were in those early years?" Her throat was tight.

"No," said Eve, "not now."

In the quiet kitchen, Mary Kay rocked gently back and forth in her rocking chair. As the afternoon wore on, the refusal she had given Eve had come to seem arbitrary. Stung by her realization that her attitude stemmed not only from a desire to protect Eve from the communication with Scott which would most certainly ensnare her further, but also from a reluctance to involve herself in this dangerous situation, Mary Kay had been forced to reconsider.

And now she sat motionless in the yellow rocker, her eyes closed. It was becoming clear what her decision must be. For better or worse, having begun, she must continue. If there was help available, she could not refuse Eve access to it. She would try to talk to Max tonight, after the children were in bed.

"It is not a matter of this particular mortal life alone," said Scott, "but of an indefinite number of lives we shared." The planchette was moving slowly, heavily, over the board. Mary Kay felt the spreading of a congealing numbness in her extremities. For some minutes now, as the conversation had continued, she had been registering in her own nervous system the tide of emotion which swept her guest. She felt him seated across the table, and sensing his distress, yearned to reach out and place her hand upon his.

"You are familiar with the function of the Planning Group," Scott continued spelling. "It was in response to their request that Eve and I volunteered to undertake an experiment in an effort to shed light on the subject of communication between the two planes, that is to say, the nature and the effects of such communication, and, of course, in the end, to determine whether it is indeed a thing to be desired at all."

"When did all this happen?" asked Mary Kay. "Eve has never talked to you, Scott. I don't understand—"

"She has not talked to me on this board, my dear, nor in any other way, to her conscious knowledge, during the time she has been on your plane. I am referring to the period of time when we lived on my plane, before she left me to be born into mortal life."

"Wait a minute, now, Scott. You and Eve were together before she was born? I'm not sure Eve will accept that. She says she doesn't believe in reincarnation. You are talking about other lives together? That's what you mean?"

"It does not matter whether she believes. Perhaps it is as well if she does not believe. I desire only that which will permit her the greatest degree of comfort at this time. I am explaining briefly to you, for your own sake, hoping that if you understand the depth of my relationship with Eve you will find our situation somewhat more palatable."

The planchette stopped, indicating that Scott was waiting for a comment from her, but Mary Kay—torn between her resentment and disapproval of the situation to which Scott referred on one hand, and an instinctive empathy for Scott on the other hand—did not reply.

"I have been given certain recalls—memories, you might call them—of the mortal life before this, which we endured together," Scott continued.

"Endured? You mean it was an unhappy life?"

"The few recalls available to me indicate that it was a very painful one."

"Can you tell me about it?"

"I would much prefer describing our life together on this plane, my plane, after we were at last freed from that mortal existence through death of the bodies. However, mana grows short. Let me say only that for nearly half a century, as you reckon time, we shared a life of such beauty as to defy description, were there time to render it. Truly mated, in the sense of complementing each the other in all things, we lived a life mutually dedicated to God, filled with service joyfully given. Through the Higher Ones, the Planning Group, we were presented the opportunity to contribute to a work which we regarded as of supreme significance. The price was a terrible one: Eve must leave our home to take up once again a mortal body and live as long as that body should endure in earth's painful classroom. We would have certainly refused to undergo such an ordeal had it not been that the law required it, inasmuch as we had been so richly blessed that our repayment must be of equal magnitude.

"So we were parted, and on the various levels of consciousness we managed to go forward with our plan. There were no great problems until our relationship began to penetrate her conscious mind. That area and that area alone she has committed to Warner, and I must not impinge upon it. So it is ended now, and I release her so that she may live out the incarnation without my shadow upon her. She must accept this as I accept it. But because she is in need, I send her this poem as my final message:

I charge you to live out your life, my Eve,
Using your genius in whatever way you need
To make the unpalatable palatable,
The unendurable endurable,
The joyless joyful.

And when leading comes
Do not subdue the springing emotion.
For attitude is all: the opened palm
Accepts the lover's kiss
Or lets the heaped-up flowers fall,
But the closed hand presses the mouth in bitterness.
Do not be afraid to follow the song.

The room was growing cold. Although the hour was late, Kenneth added a small log to the dying fire. He would have to have a serious talk with Mary Kay, in spite of the fact that she was very tired. This thing had gone far enough.

Turning to her, he observed her carefully. She was still seated at the small table near the shaded lamp. She had pushed the board away, the sitting finally ended, and was wearily studying the scattered papers on which he had recorded the evening's conversation. The utter fatigue which followed psychic endeavor, at least in her case, was never more pronounced than it was tonight. Something was going to have to be done about it.

As always at such times, seeing her like this, he felt a stab of loving concern for her. She is so deeply involved emotionally, he thought, that there is no longer any doubt about her belief in the validity of Max and his crew. They and the strange world they inhabit have become as real to her as her own world. No use any longer trying to deny it—this bright, almost brainy girl has fallen for the lure of the occult, the supernatural scene. It had happened, what he'd always heard would happen to those who dabbled with the Quija board and such: Mary Kay was ending up some kind of a nut. And he had not only failed to protect her, he had actually egged her on. Damn.

On the other hand, he reflected, his observation of her experience over the years had convinced him that Mary Kay was not *consciously* creating that other world, that world peopled with finely drawn characters, each one consistent, growing, changing with the years but never out of character. His own choice, among the recognized possible explanations, was that through the use of the board she had tapped a direct line to her subconscious mind—admittedly a sub with a lively imagination, even a creative talent! Indeed, he was inclined to think that this was probably the case, and that this board of hers had unlocked a door more commonly opened by hypnosis, dream analysis and drugs.

"Let me fix you a brandy, hon," he said now, giving her a pat on the back of the neck as he passed her chair on his way to the kitchen.

"You know what this means," she called after him. "You know it means I can't stop." He did not answer.

In the living room, he handed her the glass and she took it absently. "Rub my back, will you please, Ken?" she asked tiredly.

"I know you're upset," he said. "You've gone and got your subconscious all in an uproar."

"I thought catharsis for the subconscious mind was supposed to make you feel better, not worse."

"That's the theory," replied Kenneth, "but you insist on believing your sub didn't make it up. That's why you're shook up."

"That's right. I believe what Max told me tonight and I'm shook up. You're one hundred percent correct, kiddo."

"I wish you could be just the least bit scientific about this."

"And I wish to God I'd never gotten mixed up in all this in the first place."

"No need to keep saying that. I'm tired of hearing it."

"I'll say it if I want to."

"Oh, Mary Kay, quit working yourself up. You ought to know better."

"Kenneth, why are you so insensitive toward me? Don't you care anything about how I feel?"

"Of course I care. That's why I don't want you

making yourself sick again over nothing but a bunch of—"

"Garbage? Let's face it, Kenneth. You don't want me to get upset or sick because if I do, then you feel guilty about wanting me to go on with all this stuff."

"Did I ask you to go on with it? Did I?"

"No, you won't ask. You never ask me outright. That might be a comfort to me, if you would ask. But no. You want me to go on because you're intrigued, you want to finish the instrument—in spite of all it's costing us—and you need my work for that. You're using me. I'm part of a project, a necessary cog in your machine, that's all I am. And if I get sick and kooky in the process, then you feel guilty about it and irked at me for messing up."

Stung by the uncomfortable accuracy of Mary Kay's assessment of his position, Kenneth rose to the attack.

"All right, quit," he said impatiently, "go ahead and quit, then. I only put up with it because it was important to you. You're always talking about being free, doing what you want to do to express individuality, following your own drummer, all that Aquarian crap. So I let you do it, I indulged you a little, and that's the thanks I get." He had to turn away from the shock and outrage in her eyes, and added warningly, though in a lower tone, "It's getting to you, Mary Kay. You're going overboard. If you keep this up—"

"Don't worry, boss, I won't keep it up. And thank you very kindly for indulging me all this time," she muttered. "And believe me, your favors can end here and now. I have problems aplenty, all this work and your monstrous children and no help and not much money and someone like you for a husband—" She wiped the tears from her hot eyes with the back of her hand and glared at him. "I have enough to handle. I'm not about to go any farther with this load of Eve's and Scott's, this mess that is liable to ruin several lives before it gets through, including mine if I let it. I've got a life to live, too. Evidently no one thinks of that, not even you. I can't shoulder all this on top of everything else I've got shoved on me."

"Drink your brandy, hon, and don't be so dramatic."

"Brandy won't help what's wrong with me. Nothing but throwing that damn board in the fireplace will do that."

She's really riled up, he said to himself. Maybe this time she means it.

"There's nothing wrong with you but nerves. Drink up, the brandy will settle you down."

But Mary Kay was really crying now. Kenneth held her on his lap while she sobbed. "Oh, Ken, how can I tell Eve what came on the board tonight? She'll want to know. I promised I'd ask Max about her trouble. What can I say? I don't want her to know. A thing like this, just think what it can do to her, through the years to come."

"She knew before, when she was here, that there was a man on that side, and about the baby that was coming. She took it all right. What's so drastic about what came through tonight?"

"Well, before, it was just the outline of the situation. It was a shock, and upset us both, but it all sounded so fantastic, it just didn't seem as *real* as it did tonight. Max's bringing Scott to me, Scott's talking to me, in his own words, in his own way, his own vibrations.... Ken, couldn't you just *feel* him there? I could almost see him. It was so real! It wasn't like a story, some science-fiction yarn that someone was trying to get us to believe—it was a real human being sitting there, his heart thumping away, his voice shaking with emotion— don't say you couldn't almost hear that? This isn't some wispy-waspy ghostie we're dealing with, this is a real, terrific man and he's very much alive."

Kenneth moved uncomfortably in the chair. He didn't like Mary Kay's raving on about this guy and besides, she was getting heavy.

"Ken, Eve can't help responding to a man like that. Any woman would. And she's married to Warner and up until now has been very much in love with him. You can see the problem shaping up. Don't pretend you don't."

Okay, here goes, he said to himself.

"Problems I see, yep, two of them. One named Eve and one named Mary Kay. I think both of you girls need to go out and get jobs, see what a real scuffle in the real world is like out there in the marketplace. Get into politics or public work of some kind, use your wits to figure out how to solve some of the honest-to-God problems of the hard world of reality. You both have too much time on your hands, too much time to manufacture fantasies, work up soap-opera crises—"

But Mary Kay had bounded out of his lap. She gave him one look of intense dislike and walked stiffly from the room, stripping her clothes from her as she went.

In the bathroom she began running water into the tub. The put-back ironing, she mused. The pre-school checkup tomorrow morning. The paint peeling on the outside window-sills, the ones that must be painted before it rained again. The caulking around the bathtub. Letters owed. Bills unpaid. The overdue Pap test. The brakes on the car— Tired, tired, tired, all the time now. And she didn't even like the children very much any more. And as for Ken—"I could kill him," she whispered angrily.

Max, she beamed to him, do I have to tell Eve? About their life together on the IM?

The hot water did not soothe her. She got out, powdered with the baby's Johnson talc, put on her worn cotton nightgown, the one that had seen her through all four pregnancies. The children—, she thought suddenly. Am I shortchanging them by my involvement with psychic work? Probably, was the gloomy answer. Then through the bathroom door she heard Kenneth's voice.

"Hon, I got a ham sandwich here. Want me to fix you one? You'd feel better if you ate."

Jerking open the door she confronted him irritably. There he stood in the hallway, his round face crinkled about the eyes in a tentative grin, his hand holding out a thick, sloppily made sandwich. Food, his panacea for all of life's ills, she thought fondly, her ire evaporating. I give up; Ken's Ken, take him or leave him. She threw herself in his arms, bouncing slightly off his rotund stomach, loving him in spite of all. "Yeah," she said, "and a glass of milk."

He pinched her a bit and took a bite of sandwich over her shoulder, dropping a few shreds of lettuce as he munched.

Warner awoke in the night, hearing Eve crying in her sleep. He turned on the bedside lamp and looked at her. She was sleeping deeply, he could tell, but the lashes that lay on the warm, damp cheek were rimmed with tears and the mouth trembled.

He had learned not to wake her at these times. That only made things worse. She acted stunned, as though someone had struck her a reeling blow. Better to let her come out of it herself. Just leave me alone, she had said. She had made him promise that.

He had also learned from experience that he would not go back to sleep again. In the kitchen he poured himself some scotch, lit a cigarette, and sat down at the breakfast table. He sighed deeply. Two nights last week, three the week before. Something was wrong with her but damned if he could figure out what. Pregnancy had never affected her in this way before. Even the one that went wrong, that was never quite right from the start and had ended in miscarriage. Even during that one she had never been like this. Why should she be so depressed, even in her sleep? It was nothing physical. They had ruled that out in the beginning.

Eve shouldn't have taken that trip to Washington. At the time, he had thought it would perk her up, but it seemed to have left her more disturbed than ever. She'd been strange for quite a while, he thought. Even before she knew about the baby. So that couldn't be what was bothering her. Or could the baby thing be part of it now? It couldn't be that she didn't want the baby. Could it? No, she wanted the baby. He could tell. There was no reason why she should be upset over the pregnancy. They had planned on having at least two more children. They could afford it. Their house was large enough, great for kids. They had designed it for a big family. And Marsalina was terrific with kids. Maybe they'd need some extra help when the baby came. If so, no problem. What, then? He had to do something. But what?

At breakfast, he looked at Eve carefully. She was absorbed in the morning paper, sipping her orange juice with apparent relish. But Warner noticed the dark circles under her eyes, and with a rush of tenderness, he saw upon her face the first signs of aging revealed in the morning light.

"Evie," he said suddenly, "let's go shopping today. I'll take the day off."

"What for?" replied Eve absently, not looking up from her paper.

"Let's get you some great-looking maternity clothes."

Now Eve raised her head and looked squarely at him, her eyes wide.

"And have lunch at the club," he added.

"When have you ever gone shopping with me for clothes? Any clothes—but especially maternity clothes!"

"Well," said Warner, "I thought you might like me to."

"You never thought so before. The other times, I mean."

"This is different."

"Different how?"

"I don't know exactly. You seem to be taking it differently."

Eve was silent for a moment. "I know it's different, Warner," she said gravely. "But I'm not a spoiled, ungrateful child, and you don't need to coddle or placate me. Really, you don't. You're a wonderful person, Warner, and I know it, and I love you. You don't have to keep trying to prove it. But thanks, anyway."

Driving to the office, he thought of her lovingly.

What a great gal she was! Of all the good things in life that he had, she was the greatest. Maybe a weekend, away somewhere, just the two of them, would fix her up.

IM-level

"This room," thought Eve, "will I remember it? The fireplace, the little supper table, the ivory-canopied bed. . . ?" It was, she knew, their last night together while her mortal incarnation lasted. This was the end of nightly pleas and protests, availing nothing. There was nothing left to be said. Scott was unshakable in his resolve, and she would petition him no more.

"I am leaving now, Scott," she said clearly. "Only remember that it is because of you that I will not be coming again."

"I pray you, Beloved, do not leave me in anger," said Scott, anguished, taking her into his arms.

Eve stood motionless within his embrace. "You are the one who is doing this thing to me, and to Matthew," she answered.

"I do it in love," he said, "and for your sake."

"I cannot recognize a love like that," Eve said.

Suddenly her aura blazed scarlet. "My son—I still have time to see my son for the last time."

"We will go to him together," he said, still holding her.

"No," she said, "I will say goodbye to him alone."

Slowly, her mana ebbing, she made her way to the nursery wing and through the beaded draperies to the place where his crib stood. Matthew slept in his familiar baby posture, his arms upflung, his chubby little fists curled tight. Looking down at him, Eve felt a slow leaking of her life force. The silver cord was thinning, spinning out, almost a thread, a cobweb thread. There was no more time. The mortal body drew her, and soon the darkness would begin, and then her exile.

Stumbling now, she passed into the corridor, and when she stopped upon the staircase, her vision dim, he was beside her, holding her.

"Scott, oh, Scott, I beg you. Don't send me away."

"I must, my heart's darling," he replied, his eyes burning in his ashen face.

"I can never forgive you, Scott."

"Even so," he answered.

As the darkness claimed her, Eve caught a last glimpse of the valley, and the river Jupiter, gliding, gliding. She could not see the hills beyond.

"I can hate as passionately as I have loved," she said. If he replied, she could no longer hear. The cord was almost invisible now.

It was ended.

PART FOUR

Yes! We'll gather at the river!
　—the beautiful—
　　　—beautiful—
　　　　　river!
Gather with the saints
　　　at the river!
　　　　—that flows by the throne of God.

M-level

As the summer neared an end, Eve began to feel a sense of hope. Soon the intense heat would lift from the San Fernando valley, and then before too long a time, perhaps, the rain would come. It seemed to her that with the rain would come relief for her own spirit as well as for the land, which now lay exhausted, limp with dust, under the searing ordeal of the heat wave. She could hold out until then, she told herself. Even now, the prospect of surcease had brought with it a feeling of returning control. Surely she was getting better. The acute distress that had been with her during the early months of her pregnancy had passed about the time of

Mary Kay's visit. How grateful she had been for those few days! And how like Mary Kay to come to her, at Warner's call, when she had almost lost the baby that first time! The taxi had drawn up about the same time Eve had arrived home from the hospital. Mary Kay had been embarrassed and apologetic because she had had to bring her youngest child with her and the baby had been airsick and had thrown up all over them both, and she had said her hair was a mess but there had been no time to fix it, things had happened so fast, and her clothes were all wrong for California. But Eve had been overwhelmed with joy and the comfort of being with her again. Every day, every hour, was precious. They had spent as much time as they could with each other and with Max. They had begrudged the time it took for the rituals of eating, of sleeping, of attending to the routine amenities of daily living. And then Mary Kay was waving goodbye with the baby's hand, the plane lifted off, and Eve was alone again.

No. Not really alone. Certain memories remained, remote, peripheral, but always there. Always.

Of course it was a good thing the episode with Scott was ended. She could see that. It had been a bizarre experience, the Scott thing. He had seemed as vivid to her as Max, and she had responded to him in the strangest way. It was like being in another world, a world where Warner and the children did not exist at all, a world where Scott was real and nothing else was real and it was perfectly all right for her to feel as Scott felt. It was so . . . But naturally, it could not go on. Mary Kay was right about that. Maybe it really had disturbed her enough to contribute to her near miscarriage, as Mary Kay had said. In any case, it was best that it was over. And anyway, she had never really believed it in the first place, she told herself.

She had plunged into a time of intense devotion to her family. She had never appreciated Warner more, and she tried to show him her love in every possible way. The children ... ah, the children! She had taken over their care entirely, loath to leave even the most trivial concern of theirs to Marsalina. Everything had seemed so much better, so nice and normal. Until the evening of their anniversary. Warner had brought home his gift to her, the crystal goblets. Unaccountably, just at that moment she had begun to tremble, and by midnight Warner had taken her back to the hospital again.

But that was all over now. Well, the nights were still quite bad. But Warner no longer worried about it. When she cried out or wept in her sleep, he just awakened her as gently as he could and they didn't even discuss it. Only a few weeks to go now before the baby was due. It would be all right. She was in control. She would make it.

It was just that sometimes ... not often, just once in a while ... her control would break, and all for no reason, either. Just something like a sound, a certain shadow shape, a color of mountain or a stone, a drift of music ... just things like that, and then the feeling, like bleeding, would begin. All due to the vagaries of pregnancy, she supposed. All of it, the poems that rose in the night ... all. Well, it would soon be over.

IM-level

Running along the path to the woodland, Harriet tried to direct an intense concentration toward Robert, in the way he was teaching her to do. It was called "flashing," he had said, and you did it by picturing the person you wanted to reach. It was really fantastic, she thought happily, once you caught on to how to do it.

Mocking up Robert's face, she felt her usual rush of admiration. Robert was really great-looking. He'd said he'd been here for three hundred years or more, but how could he look so young? His heavy black hair was long, it hung to his shoulders, his face was smooth and of a beautiful soft brown color, and his teeth flashed white and his eyes were always sending out smiles.... It worked! Seeing him so clearly in her mind, she suddenly knew where he was. Robert was in his private place in the forest where his altar stood. He had taken her there once when she had first come to Scott's house to live. Robert worshipped the Sun God there. He said the Sun God was the same as her God, really. But how could that be? What a strange place this was, anyway! No matter how much you learned, there was always something else to try to figure out, to try to understand. Even Robert was still learning. He'd said he was learning about love; that it was hard for him to let himself love because something bad always happened to people he loved.

Coming into the glade, Harriet saw Robert walking toward her, his arm raised in greeting. He had finished with his prayers. He wore a long cape of yellow feathers, and she could see that he was naked under it. He was so cute and funny and sweet—half savage and half English butler! Suddenly she began to run faster, running toward him, running to Robert, her Robert, her strange Robert.

Robert caught her hands, smiling, holding her at arm's length as she came closer and attempted to throw her arms about him.

"What's the matter?" she said, "Why won't you hold me?"

"You must not touch the cape," he replied, still smiling.

"Why not?" demanded Harriet. "Let me touch it, Robert."

"No, Harriet, I cannot. The cape is holy. It is my prayer cape."

"Oh, Robert," she cried, strangely hurt, "it's only a bunch of feathers. Don't be silly."

Robert did not reply. He continued to gaze at her fresh young face and the clear eyes that were widening now with distress.

Harriet was suddenly swept with loneliness. Unaccountably, she began to cry. "I want to get inside the cape, Robert," she wept.

"No," said Robert. "That I cannot permit."

"Don't shut me out," she protested. "You're under that cape, so I want to be under there, too. Let me under that cape, I tell you!" She reached for the cape with both hands. Robert stepped aside.

"Harriet, my dear little Harriet," he said, smiling no longer. "Do not force me to dissolve the cape. I cannot allow you to touch it."

"I don't understand," she said desolately. "Why can't I? You act like I would contaminate it or something."

"It is that the cape is not holy to you."

"No," said Harriet, "the cape is not holy to me. *You* are what is holy to me. But the cape is holy to you. That's why I want to wear it, too."

Bertram arrived early at Ida's house. It was to be one of their informal little dinners alone together, and since he had been feeling a bit undone of late, he looked forward to a restful hour before dining. When he entered the tall, doorless entry he did not see Ida about, and with the ease of long familiarity he passed through the softly lighted foyer, cool with its patterned tiles and lush green plantings, past the doorway to the salon, its carpet pale against the walls of ruby light, and on down the corridor to Ida's sitting room. Making himself comfortable upon a small and deeply padded sofa covered with embroidered linen, Bertram removed his shabby sweater and stretched his legs. He gave a sigh of pleasure. How many times in this small room the two of them had worked into the night, dissecting, sometimes solving, always relishing the problems Ida brought to him from her day's work at Minds Analysis. Always there was her bright face, alive with interest, the glowing fire, the sandwiches and scalding tea which they consumed while sitting on the floor when work was through, their papers strewn about and quite forgotten as they talked.

Through the open doorway he saw Ida hurrying down the corridor toward him and he rose to greet her. He noticed that she was dressed rather absentmindedly in what appeared to be a half-finished hostess gown. With both arms raised, she was tying back her hair at the nape of the neck, in the way she wore it at the office. Bertram felt a constriction in his heart as he looked at her fondly. How she had changed since he had first seen her! A frightened girl in her early twenties she had been, frantic with rebellious fury at being suddenly cut off from the life she knew and loved. She was a lovely young woman now, maturity having developed in her a unique combination of tough-minded courage and delicate insight, a combination that made her invaluable in her post in Minds Analysis. Yes, she could carry on his work after he had gone, maybe even better than he had, himself.

"Oh, good, you got away early," she said, hugging his arm affectionately. "I look a mess, but no matter. Come, have a glass of wine with me."

"Champagne?" he asked, smiling, knowing her propensity for it.

"No," she said, surprisingly. "This isn't a champagne occasion."

On the terrace, Ida faced him across the small table. "Let's not fool around, Bertram. You've accepted the contract, haven't you?" And then, receiving his unspoken answer, she raised both open palms in supplication. "Oh, Bertram," she said faintly, "just tell me why. That's all I want to know. For God's sake, why?"

"It's simple, Ida. I need to make another trip."

"You don't want to go into the M-level again! You've already admitted that."

"I want to go, dear child. But you are right—I dread the experience."

"Of course you dread it! Doesn't everybody?"

"No, not everyone."

"Well, I would."

"Yes, I know."

Bertram patted her hand in an effort to comfort her.

The affectionate gesture seemed to have the reverse effect. Ida got to her feet and began to walk about the terrace, agitatedly.

"So—the Planning Group has sold you a bill of goods, Bertram, and you've fallen for it, that's what it amounts to!"

"I haven't fallen for anything. My mission is sacrificial."

"Oh Lord! The M-level needs another martyr? What towering contribution do you plan to make? You think you are going to revolutionize psychiatry in the mortal world?"

"My contract requires only that I try."

"Couldn't hurt," Ida said sagely, shrugging her shoulders. "But look what's happened to others who've tried it! No kidding, is that really in the contract?"

"I must promise to try to make significant advances in mental health. The Group does not promise that I will succeed."

"Sure," said Ida resentfully, "when do *they* ever promise anything?" Bertram did not answer. "You know I filed a report of protest, soon as I heard about this," she told him. "I haven't had a reply."

"Ida, I want you to withdraw that report," said Bertram firmly.

"No."

"Dear child, don't resist the Planning Group. Learn that, now, before you bring suffering upon yourself."

"Why do you say that? They don't punish anybody."

"I say it because they know best. They have access to more knowledge. They are closer to God."

"Oh, Bertram, I don't care if they are. Don't go. Just tell them nothing doing."

"I cannot."

"Don't be afraid of them. Just refuse to go along with them. Thank them for their advice and decline to take it, the way Scott did."

"Ida," he said earnestly, "Scott has made a serious mistake."

"Oh, come on, Bertram," cried Ida, "we all have free will. Scott is acting in line with standards he acquired in a perfectly legitimate way—in one of their precious incarnations. How else would you expect an unreconstructed Victorian to feel?"

"Darling, you must see that Scott's error is in placing his judgment above that of the Higher Ones, the Planning Group."

Ida sat speechless, regarding him hopelessly. "I don't know, Bertram," she said finally. "I guess you've progressed so far I can't understand you any more. Maybe you do need another trip, at that."

"That's right," he said, patting her hand and smiling. "Don't resist life so, Ida."

"Some life," she smiled, rising and holding out both hands to him. "Sometimes I almost wish I were dead. Let's have dinner."

"Scott," said Joel Higgins, seating himself in the armchair and placing his portfolio across his knees, "I have a communication for you from the Planning Group."

"I've been expecting it," replied Scott. "I realize I am in violation of my contract."

"I'm afraid it is more serious than that, my friend," said Higgins, opening his case and withdrawing a sheet of paper which he extended to Scott. "It was for this reason I asked to call on you without delay. I received this message during the night, after some hours of prayer and meditation. I believe it to be as accurate as it is possible for psychic reception to be."

Taking the single sheet in his hand, Scott considered. Almost, he was inclined to refuse to read it. What did it matter now, the stern warning which he was certain it contained? He had made his decision in full awareness of the consequences of breaking even a part of his pledge.

"Read it, Scott," said Joel earnestly. "It concerns Eve, too."

Scott glanced up quickly at Higgins and then, slowly and reluctantly, began to read.

After Joel Higgins had taken his leave, Scott returned to the library. He was suddenly aware that the room depressed him. Always before, he had enjoyed its air of informal intimacy, now seemingly transformed into a cramped and shrunken shabbiness. And the light, once softly warm, now shed a listless dimness all about—an accurate reflection of his consciousness, Scott thought.

The brandy decanter still stood upon the low table by the dying fire, and dropping into his chair, Scott poured the amber liquid into his glass, but the sight did not please, nor, as he sipped, did the brandy cheer.

It was decided, and he felt no regret. He would bring Eve home, as the Group had advised. No other course was possible now, he realized. Once more, in what was left of their home, he would attempt to show her the irreversible rightness of his view that they must remain parted for the duration of her mortal life. But recalling with anguish the final words between them, and her bitter wrath, Scott knew that what Higgins had revealed was true, that such potent repressed emotion was reflecting itself upon the helpless child she bore, imperilling its very mortal life, and as for what influence had been made upon its psyche, none could estimate.

Her feelings of rejection, of being controlled by a decision made by another, a decision with which she was not in agreement, her feelings of hopelessness and despair, all these had been forcibly submerged, driven deep into the subconscious area of her mind where no expression of them was possible in sufficient measure. Her effort to sublimate grief and rage through excessive devotional service, through overvaluing Warner and through conscious effort to cease believing in Scott's existence, all these attempts were insufficient to quench the destructive fire.

Yes, he would bring her home, for one short, precious time, and in those hours he would impart to her Joel's message. She would understand that her bitterness must be resolved for the child's sake. When she left him, she would leave comforted in her full understanding and in their abiding love.

The hour was late but before he left he must notify Max of the step he intended to take. He flashed, but Max did not reply at once. He is sleeping, Scott thought. When at length Max answered, Scott spoke briefly. Max made one terse comment—"Big of you!"—and cut off.

Scott made his way up the curving staircase to their bedroom. He must make preparation for Eve's coming, and loath to disturb Robert at this hour, he set about the task himself. Matthew would still be sleeping when she came, so nothing need be done for him; but as he surveyed their bedroom he saw that he would not be able, unassisted, to return it to its normal order and richness. For some time now he had been dully aware of the gradual deterioration of the household furnishings. The beauty which had been produced and sustained by harmony and loving attention had been fading away, dissolving, as a result of his preoccupation with discord. He attempted to remove the crumpled sheet from the bed where he had tossed in restlessness, but he could not concentrate enough to do so. Eve's desk was bare, even the silver vase had long since evaporated. Yet, oddly, he now saw the vase materialize again, filled with her favorite white lilacs in extravagant profusion. His urgency had thrown his creative processes in disarray. He could not collect himself for such work, distraught as he was.

Giving it up in dismay, he prepared to project himself to Eve. She would be sleeping, waiting as he knew she still waited nightly, despite it all.

But as he stood upon the patio of her house, groping toward her with his force, he knew that she was not asleep. He felt his mind connect with hers, and grief smote him like a blow. She was in pain. The pain would not let her sleep.... He could not lift her in his arms and take her home!

But he could not leave her. She would not even know that he had come to her. How could he help her now? He could not help. But nevertheless, he could not leave her, would not leave her.

"My heart's darling," he cried out. "Beloved!"

In his distraction he did not at first believe that she had heard him. He saw her coming, ah, slowly in her pain, her flowing robe swelling where the child lay waiting. Her heavy hair, pale in the half-light before the dawn, rippled in disarray around her shoulders. His force blazed from him, leaving him almost unsupported, covering her, entering her, merging with her.

"Look at me!" he demanded, desperately. "See me!" But he knew she could not see him.

M-level

In pain, timing her contractions, Eve had risen at last from her bed, and moving quietly, not to awaken Warner, had slipped through the dark and sleeping rooms to the patio, cool in that pre-dawn hour.

Below the balustrade the valley sprawled, unfamiliar in the early half-light, misted, for one strange moment, in an ancient beauty. A sensation as of memory tugged at her mind—quickly, feebly, and was gone. Suddenly Eve was swept by a longing of such enormity that she sank into the lounge, unable to stand.

"Oh ..." she pleaded, but whether she spoke aloud she did not know.

Comfort spread so slowly through her that at first she was not aware that she was quieted.

In her mind, very clearly and all at once, like a line from one of her poems, a word formed: Shenandoah.

For one instant she nearly saw him standing beside the lounge where she lay, and then, unmistakably, she felt his hand pass over her hair in a gesture of tenderness. As she felt the sudden rush of tears spill over, she almost expected to sense his fingers wiping them away, but there was nothing....

And now as the sun began to pale the east, the line of mountains took shape beyond the valley where the city lay. The air was very still. Another contraction seized her, and when it had passed she rose from the lounge and went, quite steadily now, into the house to awaken Warner. It was time for the child to be born.

IM-level

Bertram stood looking out the wide windows of Ida's office. The valley appeared faintly misted to his sight, and the outlines of the walkways which led from the building seemed to him blurred, the flower borders indistinct.

Ida had not spoken for some time. She was sitting quietly enough at her desk, apparently engrossed in going through the papers he had brought to her for her signature. Still, he dared not look at her. He had put all his affairs in order save this one task and he had put it off until last, unable to do otherwise. Now he must no longer procrastinate. She would sign the articles of agreement which they had mapped out together, concerning her stewardship of his manuscripts and notes. He would then turn over to his successor all the accoutrements accumulated in the course of his work throughout the years. It would be finished.

At last he heard her voice but he did not turn to face her.

"I guess that's got it, doll," she was saying. "Listen, this is it, isn't it?"

Bertram was silent.

"I'm not going to carry-on," she continued, her voice tight. "I don't want to make it any harder on us than . . ." She could not go on.

At last he turned and looked at her—her pale face, the brilliant eyes—for the last time. "I am to enter the monastery tonight," he said.

"And after devotions, then will . . . Bertram, will it be an anaesthetic?"

"No, Ida, it will be samadhi."

"What's that?"

"You might understand it as a form of trance. While I'm waiting, you know."

"Oh, Bertram," and her voice broke, "help me do a good job of this. Just go. Let's not try to talk."

"You're right," he said, turning his eyes away. "Well, then, every good wish, Ida."

"Have a good trip." She tried to smile but the tears gushed forth instead.

Unsteadily he made his way to the door. She rose from her chair but she did not follow him. Bertram closed the door softly.

The hall stretched before him, brightly lit with daylight. He shaded his eyes with his hand to avoid the glare. His mana was running low, he thought. It seemed a long way to the end of the hall to his office door.

Ida made her way unsteadily into the bath, trying hard to mock up a privacy screen at the doorway. The pool seemed strangely distant, and when she reached its rim, she clung to the railing as she stepped into the tepid water. In the mirrored walls she saw with a sense of shock that her body appeared shadow-like, sheer, almost transparent. Unbelieving, she sought to press her palms upon her breast.

For the past several hours, as she lay awake in bed, she had been aware of a crushing fatigue, and she had known that her body was seriously depleted of mana. She had made an effort to recharge, but no answering surge of vitality had come. At last she had risen and sought the tranquility of the falling waters. Now, however, having grasped the full significance of her condition, she felt a rising panic. Never before had she been like this. What if she could not stop the mana leak? What if—? When Bertram goes, she thought, it is in this way that he will destroy his body as he prepares to enter the new body on the M. He will simply stop recharging.

Standing in the pool, letting the waterfall stream over her, she petitioned, as she had been taught: Fill me! But there was no reply.

"Max!" she flashed, "Help me! Hurry!" Was there enough power behind the flash to wake him? she wondered frantically, but then, to her relief, she saw him coming from the bedroom.

Toward morning, Max had wakened suddenly. A faintly luminous mist pervaded the bedroom. Alarmed, he sat up in bed, instinctively turning to Ida. In the grey distress light, which he had seen so often on the battlefield when working there, he could tell that she was gone. Hastily he followed the line of concentrated light. She was in the bathing room. Remembering her hopeless grief of the night before and the marked depletion of her vital energy, he hurriedly made his way toward her. She had thrown up a privacy screen across the archway and he penetrated it with difficulty.

In the bath pool he saw her standing beneath the waterfall, her body almost transparent, sagging as if with illness. Appalled by the translucence of her form, Max ran headlong into the pool, catching her against him.

"Darling, what is it? Ida, I'm here. Ida!"

When she did not answer, Max lifted her, carrying her, water streaming from them both, across the marble floor. A chaise had been pulled up close to the pool and Max fell onto it, supporting her upon the length of his body. Could this be Ida, the indomitable Ida, now so dangerously depleted of mana? "For God's sake, why didn't you recharge?" he demanded, incredulous.

She was lying still in his arms, her eyes closed to him. He could not tell whether she heard him. Strands of her long wet hair fell about her cheeks and he brushed them away, distractedly, and pressed his face to hers. Probing for her attention, he could detect no response, and in desperation he began to beam into her aura his own vital force, the sacred mana. He could not feel her receiving it. When at last her eyes opened, large and dark in her pale face, she struggled to speak.

"Not yet, Ida darling. Don't talk yet," he urged. "I'm beaming to you. Wait, try to take it from me. Don't focus on Bertram any more. That's what's doing this to you—"

"I don't think I can stand it," she whispered.

"Yes you can, Ida. Baby, listen to me. This is the first time you've been through this particular hell. The first time it's come this close. The first time someone you really love has gone back to the M. I know it's hard for you. But you'll get used to it."

"No." She looked into his eyes. "No," she said again.

"I did, after a while. So will you. You'll see. The grief will begin to ease up."

"It's like death, isn't it, Max? Worse than death."

"No, it's not like that at all, Ida. You know that. You'll be seeing Bertram again. Maybe quite often."

"But it won't be *Bertram*. Not the Bertram we know."

Tears welled in her eyes, and as they did so, it seemed to Max that there was a sudden blurring of the outlines of her face. Trying not to show his concern, he said gently but with as much firmness as he could muster, "Ida, don't think about it now, baby. You're leaking mana and it's got to stop."

"I can't help it."

"You've got to. I can't bear to see you like this."

"Don't I have a right to grief?"

"Not when it drains you like this."

"... still human ..."

"Ida," Max closed his eyes in concentration, reaching for her attention. "Don't try to talk. Get your mind on me. Think of me, darling. Listen to me. Focus on me."

He lay holding her closely as she lay, light and tenuous, upon him. After a time she began to stir against him, sighing. The emergency passed, he yielded himself to the great wash of tenderness that swept over him as he lay silent and spent, knowing she was being filled.

Wrapped in a huge towel, Ida sat, propped against pillows, on Max's couch. Her body had regained its normal appearance of solidity, Max noted, but studying her aura he could see the constricted inner pattern, much too pale in color.

"Come on, Ida," he said with a note of irritation. "You've got to recharge. You aren't even trying."

Ida opened her eyes and regarded him sullenly. "I don't feel like it," she replied flatly, turning her head away and closing her eyes again.

"Keep this up and you'll really be sick." Max crossed the room and attempted to stand her on her feet, but she pushed him away weakly and turned her back, pressing her face into the pillow.

"I *am* sick. Sick about everything."

"Your emotional tone is low," observed Max.

"How'd you guess?"

"It's all a matter of attitude."

There was no answer. Max tried again. "You are seeing everything negatively and that's what's blocking your flow of mana. You know that!"

"Everything *is* negative, and stop pretending it isn't."

"Listen, baby, just because everything isn't the way you want it doesn't make it negative."

"Stop trying to sound like Dr. Forbes. You aren't the type."

Max lifted her forcibly from the couch and held her to him. "Ida." She would not look at him. "We've been all through this. Bertram *wants* to go. He sees it as an opportunity. The only thing wrong with it is that you want him here."

"Well," said Ida, "Bertram, yes. But what about Eve and Scott? You can't whitewash what's happening to them."

"Ida, if you had control, if you were stage-managing their lives, what would you have happening?"

Turning away from him, Ida wrapped the towel more tightly about her. "That's what's so terrible. There's no solution for them, not now. The mistake was made when she left Scott to reincarnate in the first place. She should have stayed..."

"It won't last forever. She'll be back when it's over."

"Yes, and so will Bertram, but neither one will be the same."

"Is that important," asked Max, "compared to the Experiment?"

Whirling, Ida faced him, her aura blazing. "There you've hit it, dammit!" she cried. "There's the whole thing—the goddamn Experiment! It's monstrous, that's what it is! I wish I'd never heard of Project Jupiter, let alone worked so hard on it all these years. I hate the whole reincarnation thing! And the communication thing is just as bad! All it does is cause trouble, all this back-and-forth between the planes!"

Max looked at her, not speaking.

"Well, that's what messed it up for Eve, *communication*. Scott should have left her alone, as long as he let her go back for another trip. Now she's stuck with the whole dreary, guilty bit, and he is cutting her off—"

"She will adjust."

"How can you be so shallow?" Ida stormed. "I'll tell you one thing, if this baby is damaged because of Scott's stubbornness, she won't adjust to that!"

"Ida, be reasonable. It's not stubbornness, it's conscience."

"Look, Max. This baby is contracted. If it's damaged, the Incomer may reject the infant body. Eve will lose her baby. That's the point."

"It will be all right, darling."

"What all right?" she flashed. "In the hospital twice, having pains every few days, all this subliminal stress—and you say *all right*!"

"Eve and the baby will both be restored emotionally," said Max, in what he hoped was a calm manner, "because the Group has intervened with Scott on the child's behalf."

"When did this happen? You mean you've known this and didn't tell me? You just let me stew over it?" Ida charged.

"Joel called on Scott last night after Eve started having pains again. I got the flash during the night. I would have told you but you were asleep.'"

"Is Scott—?"

"Yes. His conscience will permit him to see Eve, for the baby's sake, Joel said."

"Just see her? You mean he won't change his mind?"

"Right."

"Just enough to take the edge off for her, is that it?" she asked, her voice tight. "A little anaesthetic so she can brace up and make it through, I guess—right, Max? And that will give the baby every advantage, and that's what's important, isn't it? Because the baby is going to be something special to the Experiment."

"Yes," Max said, "that's it, and why not? I thought you'd be glad."

"And never mind about Eve, once she gets the job done—right?" asked Ida, struggling to control her voice.

She walked stiffly into the bedroom and flung herself face-down upon the bed.

Max lay full-length beside her, attempting to place his hands on her nerve centers, but she beat him off with her fists. "What do you think you're doing!" she shouted. "—at a time like this!"

"I'm only trying to settle your aura. It's whirling. Come on, darling, let me help you."

"You stay the hell out of my aura!" she cried, and then uncharacteristically started to sob. "You've changed. I don't even know you, like this," she wept. "You're getting like Joel and all the rest of the nuts at the office."

"No," said Max, "I'm only getting a little broader view of how it all works."

"And 'Oh, how developed you're getting,' is that it? So pretty soon it's time for a trip for *you*, maybe? Will Joel come knocking on *your* door, with a long face," and she twisted her body to him, holding him frantically, "to offer you an 'opportunity,' Max?"

"Don't be ridiculous," Max said, kissing her tear-streaked face. "The Group wouldn't offer me a contract. I haven't been here long enough."

"But if they did? If they do, when the time comes, would you take it? Would you go?" She was very still now, her face pressed against his, her eyes tightly shut, waiting.

"You're kidding," he laughed. "Nothing could make me go back to that plane."

She did not speak or move.

"Are you satisfied now?" He shook her gently. "That's why you got sick over Bertram, isn't it? Because maybe it could happen to me? Don't worry. Never in a million years."

She began to cry again, but quietly. "Max," she whispered against his lips, "that's exactly what Bertram said, not a year ago."

They held each other silently. After a time she slept.

Max lay, not sleeping, holding her, until the flash came that it was time to dress and go to the office. There was work awaiting him that only he could do, and he must go.

In the pearling light of early dawn, Robert surveyed the terrace, noting with dismay its neglected state. The flagstones were still there, though thinning badly and of a muddy hue, but the plantings, the marble urns, the small fountain, had all disappeared. Failing the steady flow of force which had created them and which was necessary in order to maintain their visible forms, they had one by one become transparent, then mistlike, their outlines blurred, and then they had faded from view. There remained the two graceful lounge chairs where Scott and Eve had sat on so many bright evenings to watch the blazing stars, and still in place was the small table where Robert had—so often and with such pleasure—served their evening meal.

Scott sat there now alone, his face turned to the valley view where Jupiter, the broad river, ran silver against the darkness of the massive hills. Unable to bring himself to allow Scott to be alone with his melancholy, Robert approached to speak, but as he neared he could sense the slight resistance of the privacy screen about the chair, and turned away into the house.

Within, the same bareness and desolation lay. Gone were the intricately woven carpets, and where they had spread, the cold floor lay dull and uneven, the parquet pattern indistinct.

He had managed, out of his own vital energy, to preserve the draperies, admiring regularly and with intense concentration, their curving sweep and heavy fall, their soft blue luster. Certain furnishings, too, he had salvaged with his appreciation—the gleaming dining table, the deep chairs, the console table, also, which Eve had cherished in a special way. But no more the crystal, the silver, the tapestries and the silk hangings, which for so long had mirrored Scott's consciousness, its balance and its harmony. All gone, now, the beauty they had shared, and sharing, had sustained.

However, curiously, there were traces of Eve's presence left, a sweater tossed upon the terrace rim, her parasol on a hall table, a velvet robe upon the fireside chair in their bedroom. Scott must have retained these tokens of her, through treasuring those memories which clung to them.

When Robert reached Harriet's room, she was just coming awake. She sat up in bed and held out her arms to him. He held her with a sudden fierceness, savoring the blithe rhythm of her aura, rested, rosy with happiness. Her hands held his face, and her eyes, widened slightly with surprise, searched his.

"What is it, Robert?"

"I love you," he said.

"Yes," she said, drawing him down upon the bed. "Tell me how much, though."

"Enough for anything," he replied, his throat tight.

"Oh, Robert, something is wrong. What's happened? I can tell it's something."

"Never leave me," he said, holding her.

"Honey, what is it?" Harriet, alarmed by his urgency, struggled to rise.

"No." He held her fast. "It's only sunrise. Stay with me a little longer."

"Is Matthew awake yet?"

"Not yet. Stay ... a little longer," he repeated, his face pressed against her hair.

"Goodness, Robert," she protested, freeing herself. "I'm only going to Matthew. I had him dream his mother would be here when he woke up. Is Eve here yet?"

"Eve is not here," he replied, his voice still unsteady, "nor will she be coming. I do not know the reason why Scott did not bring her, but I know that at this moment he is sitting on the terrace, and that he is alone—quite, utterly and completely, alone."

"I knew something was wrong." Harriet was on her feet now, reaching for her robe. "Matthew will need me." She kissed him quickly and was gone.

Robert continued to reflect. Why had Eve not come to be with Scott, as planned? Was there trouble with Eve's condition? With the child's? Throughout the centuries since they three had left the ancient island homeland, Scott and Eve had often faced adversity, sometimes together, once apart, but always much involved with the dangerous mortal plane. Now, once again, Robert was unable to prevent their suffering.

How much better, how much safer, he thought, to avoid the mortal altogether, as he himself had determined to do! Was not the goal a life of unity with God? Was not the pursuit of spiritual progress better served by prayer and meditation, by peace and by harmony, all so much more easily maintained on this level?

Still, he knew, the mortal level drew, enticed, entrapped. Many could not resist its appeal, its challenge. One day Harriet would be drawn, be torn from him ... like Eve, a willing martyr to some distant cause. ...

He cast his eyes across the river to the darkness there. He could not look upon the mountains ... dared not ... lest he see the cruel cliff....

Joel Higgins waited in the hall outside the doors of the labor room. He surveyed the activity about him with a sense of compassion. The M-level consistently depressed him and for this reason he returned to it only when absolutely mandatory in the course of his work. How difficult life was for these gallant mortals for whom the simplest mechanics of survival required such effort! Their mortal span began with trauma, ended with trauma, and between these two points stretched a never-ending series of crises, great and small. A faint twinge of guilt accompanied his involuntary conclusion: none save a courageous and dedicated seeker of truth would brave this experience voluntarily. Would he, himself?

Hastily, Joel shifted his attention to the process taking place within the labor room. He had supervised the Incoming on countless occasions and it was his custom to be present inside the room with the other professionals. In this case, however, because of his personal relationship with Eve, some sense of delicacy had caused him to remain outside the room until he was needed.

It would have been so much easier, he thought, if this particular Incoming had followed some other pattern from out of the great variety of possibilities—if, for instance, the Incomer had made entry at the moment of conception, as had been deemed desirable in Matthew's case. But just as the death experiences of mortals differ in many ways, so also their reincarnating experiences differ, each Incoming being tailored to the unique requirements of the Incomer. Of all the Incoming patterns, he fretted, the one being followed in this case caused him the most distress—when the Incomer must wait until the time of birth before a determination could be made as to whether the fetus met the specifications.

Considering this case, he again reproached himself for becoming emotionally involved. If it went badly with the child, Joel's duty would be so difficult that he wondered whether it would be possible for him to carry it out. For the hundredth time he reviewed the available data, searching for justification for saving the child, should the necessity arise.

This incoming soul was designated for an unnamed service to the Experiment, and would require not only an adequate physical vehicle but also a stable psyche, both of which must meet certain specifications. Joel's function was to assess the condition of both the newborn body and of the psyche, and to determine the advisability of the entity's making a firm and final commitment to a mortal existance. This judgment, which he would flash to the Planning Group, would weigh heavily in their decision. This monumental responsibility was the only aspect of his work which consistently cost him mental suffering. To play such a part in the life of one for whom he entertained personal sensibilities of an affectionate and tender nature made his task almost overwhelming.

The unpalatable facts were not to be avoided: the fetus had been subejcted to a constant assault of negative stimuli arising from the subconscious emotional stress of the mother. The possible effects upon the physical fetus would become apparent when he performed his aura-scan immediately after birth; any damage to the psyche would be revealed to some extent then, also. In the event that the newborn child had sustained damage sufficient to make a favorable judgment impossible, then his duty was clear. He must recommend that the incoming soul reject the infant body and permit it to perish. To recommend that a soul become imprisoned in a vehicle patently unsatisfactory for the requirements of a successful discharge of the soul's commitment was unthinkable. Conversely, a recommendation which would in all likelihood result in the loss of Eve's child in its mortal expression loomed no less deplorable.

His distress continued to deepen with each probe he projected into the labor room, and when he became aware of Max and Ida approaching, he greeted them with a warmth born of relief.

"We stopped in the waiting room to check on Warner," said Ida. "Have you been here long?"

"Yes, for some time," replied Joel. "Eve is at present under heavy medication. She—"

"Listen, Joel," Max interrupted, "how about letting me see the specifications?"

"You know that is impossible, Max," said Joel, reprovingly.

"So I'm asking you to break the rules for once! This is important to me for personal reasons, as you damn well know."

"Nevertheless," returned Joel.

"Oh, don't be such an ass, Joel," interjected Ida impatiently. "You know why Max wants to know."

"I do indeed. He would like to influence my recommendation."

"Right," admitted Max, "and why not? I'm in a position to know more about the prognosis than you are. You hardly know Eve."

"My recommendation will concern the child, not Eve."

"Yes, but you can't make a decision without taking Eve into consideration."

"I must," said Joel with an edge of resentment, "and if I may say so, Max, I find it extremely odd that you should attempt to presume upon our friendship in a matter involving my work."

"Some friendship, if you call this a presumption!" said Ida. "And anyhow, you know you go through hell every time you have to file a negative report. I should think you'd be glad to have Max's insight on Eve."

Joel, making another probe, did not reply.

"If you ask me," said Harriet, "I think you've got to talk to Scott."

They were preparing Matthew for bed. Robert watched abstractedly as she bathed the baby. Matthew, as usual, wanted to play in the water and objected strenuously to having his face washed, but Harriet, determined, was coping dexterously with his flailing arms and ducking, dodging head. This nightly contest of wills ordinarily brought a chuckle of amusement to Robert. Now, however, he felt a prick of irritation at the child, but because he was attempting to focus on Scott and thus any distraction at all would have annoyed him, he did not reproach himself.

"Wait," he said, "until we can be alone. I want to

hear what you are saying but I can't concentrate on it now."

"Well, goodness, Robert, why can't you hear me? This keeps happening all the time. Everybody is always having to concentrate in this place. I can't get used to it."

In no mood for a lengthy lesson on the nature of communication on the IM-level, Robert did not answer, but went out to stand on the play-terrace off the nursery.

Surprised, Harriet hastily finished with the baby and hurried to the balcony where Robert stood apparently surveying the river, silent in the near-dark of late twilight.

Flinging her arms about him, she pressed against him in a rush of tenderness. "Okay," she said, "now concentrate."

Robert held her, but with an absentmindedness which was strange to her. "Hey," she said, "don't leave me. I want to go with you."

"I'm not going anywhere, Harriet."

"Yes you are too going somewhere! Do you think I can't tell by now when you are getting ready to project?"

"No, I'm not going."

"Yes, you have to go, Robert, you know you do. Just take me with you, that's all."

"But it may be that Scott would resent my interference, perhaps even take it as an impertinence. You must remember that he does not recall the old relationship with me."

"But haven't you told Eve and Scott who they were?

How could you be with them so long and not tell them?"

"Because it was quite some time after Scott returned to this level that I learned for certain who he was," replied Robert. "I registered in my aura the conviction that it was he. However, that did not constitute proof. I had to wait a long time before I was granted access to the records. The archives are carefully kept private. There must be sufficient reason for releasing records of former lives. When at last it was confirmed, I naturally did not reveal the truth to Scott, nor even to Eve."

"Why not? Why should the Archives keep all that secret? And why didn't you tell Eve and Scott? You told me."

"I told you because you are part of me, for one thing, and for another, you guessed, and asked if it were true, thereby opening the door, as law requires."

"But the Archives, why did they keep it secret? Oh, Robert, I don't understand how this whole thing, this whole dumb thing, works."

"One's past is a very private matter," Robert answered, smiling. "Imagine having one's past involvements and failures a matter of public record! One is better off not knowing even about oneself unless the knowledge would be of substantial help in one's present life."

"Well then, why did they finally tell you about Scott and Eve? If neither of them asked?"

"I was admitted to the archives because I felt that if my suspicions were confirmed, I could be of help to Scott and Eve. It was an acceptable motive."

"Can you find out who I was?"

"Oh, Harriet," laughed Robert, "curiosity is hardly adequate as a motive."

"Oh, well," she said. "Well, then, are you going to tell Scott who he was?"

"No, Harriet. It would have no reality for him. It would be as though he had read the story in a book. He must remember, really remember. The old memories are still there, beneath conscious awarness."

"The whole thing is crazy. I think it's just awful."

Robert did not reply. The light had gone, and on the balcony they stood close together in the darkness.

"I'm going to tell you something," said Harriet finally. "You want to know something, Robert? I don't believe any of it. You've just dreamed it all up."

"All right," he said. "It's just as well."

After a time Harriet wiped her hand across her eyes and leaned her cheek upon his shoulder. "Go ahead," she said. "Go on. Maybe you can get him to reach in to where the memories are—or else it's all a waste, everything that happened back there."

She turned away, back into the nursery. She did not look back because she knew he would be gone.

When he entered Scott's section of the house, Robert thought that perhaps Scott was not at home, for he could not register Scott's vibration. Or had Scott thrown up a privacy screen? If so, thought Robert, he must attempt to penetrate it, since the urgent nature of his call would justify such a breach of courtesy. But at length he began to sense Scott's presence, and was drawn to the atrium where he saw Scott standing beside the pool, lost in thought and unaware of Robert's approach.

Glad of the opportunity to observe Scott without his knowledge, Robert examined the aura carefully. The core was steady, burning with a white luminous power. Ah, good. But encircling the satisfactory core there flared the dark red of rebellion and around the red, another band of color, the indigo of grief.

"Scott," he called firmly, and Scott turned.

"I have come to you determined to influence your decision, if I can," said Robert, without apology.

"I made my decision long ago, before I sent her away," Scott answered. "There is no more to be said."

Robert went to stand at the wall of the parapet where, far below, the valley lay, its verdure dark and silent. The mountains, in the strange light, seemed to tower incredibly, preternaturally hulking, sharp with crags, penetrated by caverns. His eyes fixed upon the stone crests. Scott came slowly to his side and leaned on folded arms against the wall's ledge, his face pensive.

"You do not have the bearing of a man who has made a true decision, my friend," said Robert softly.

"It was my duty to decide, and I did decide."

"No," said Robert, "you acted, but there was never a decision."

Scott was silent; his eyes also had begun to search the mountainsides.

"An integrated decision brings peace, Scott," continued Robert. "You are not at peace."

Still Scott did not reply.

"You have broken your pledge," insisted Robert, "so there can be no peace."

Scott answered him heavily, "I could not in honor keep to the pledge once she became aware of me on the M-level. Surely you will grant me that."

"With whom do you feel you and Eve entered into this covenant? With the Planning Group?"

"Certainly not," retorted Scott. "I believe the Planning Group to be but an agency of God, advanced beyond us in some ways but hardly divine."

"Then to whom was the promise made?"

"It was our conviction and our intent that the promise was to God."

"A promise to do what?" persisted Robert gently.

"We made the decision together to endure our parting in order for Eve to go out, into the M, there to perform a service to which she is particularly well-fitted."

"You were told it would involve this child?"

"No. The Planning Group offered us an opportunity to undertake a mission for which Eve's basic nature made her ideally suited. Beyond that we were told nothing."

"Yet you agreed to undertake it, knowing nothing of its involvements?"

"Yes. We were willing."

"Then at what point did the chain of events begin which produced the present problem?"

"Why, I suppose it began when I brought her home to me the first night. After that time we had to continue. It seemed harmless enough, you know. We never suspected that her perception would develop so suddenly, that her life with me here would ever endanger her mission on the M-level. I must admit I was warned about the risk at the time by the Planning Group, through Joel."

"But were you forbidden to bring her here?"

"Of course not," said Scott. "The Group has no

authority to command. They merely furnish data to which they have access but which is not available to us on our level."

"And as a result of your bringing her home, Eve has begun to carry memories of you back to the M-level?"

"Whether her perception is the result of her making a life for herself on this level I do not know for certain. It is enough that she is nearing total perception, that our life here is coming closer and closer to her conscious mind."

"And you feel that her perception of this immortal life is undesirable for her?"

"It is unthinkable."

"Yet you were both willing that she end her mortal life and come to us to stay."

Scott's fist struck the balustrade. He whirled on Robert.

"Yes, damn you, you know perfectly well we were! She was part of me! She *is* part of me, has always been part of me! I never should have let her go, mission be damned! She was not contracted to her mortal family—"

"But this incoming child and Eve *are* covenanted one to the other?" Robert, though unsurprised by Scott's outburst, had stepped backward, faltering for a moment on his crippled foot. He waited until Scott was calm again and able to speak in a changed voice.

"Yes, Robert, that is the case, and she must honor that contract, in which I share responsibility. That is why our reunion was cancelled. That is why she must be free of me."

The two men paced up and down the stone paving together, saying nothing, the strange shadows moving about and above, their footfalls sounding unreal in the darkness. When Robert finally spoke, he did so slowly, almost painfully.

"Many years loom ahead for her, long years, Scott, years alone, cut off from you, from Matthew, from her real life ..."

"Her life on the M-level is very real to her."

"This is the real," replied Robert urgently. "That is the dream world, that world where you have deserted her."

Scott's steps halted. "It is not at all in the spirit of desertion that I have ended our life together here," he protested. "It is in the spirit of sacrifice, for the sake of honor."

"Still, whatever your motive, the fact remains that she *is* forsaken."

"Yes," admitted Scott. "A sacrifice is precisely that, a sacrifice."

"And you will also, perhaps, sacrifice the child who at this moment is undergoing the ordeal of birth, who is separating from a mother drained of mana by loss and grief?"

Abruptly, Scott turned away, averting his face. The eerie darkness obscured his form, but Robert pursued him to the edge of the pool where he had retreated, and stood waiting.

"If need be," Scott said at last, "yes, if need be, the child, too. There can be no compromise with the law."

"What law, Scott? In God's name, my old friend, under what law do you decree this sacrifice?"

"Why, by every law of decency and civilized behavior, by every law of honor, I know that Eve cannot love and share her life with two men simultaneously," said

Scott heatedly. "You cannot comprehend. You are still a pagan, for all your modern disguise."

"You know that I am pagan?" Robert laid his hand upon Scott's arm. "Are you beginning to remember me?" He felt Scott's arm stiffly unyielding beneath his hand. "You named me Robert," he continued earnestly. "What is my real name?"

In the changing shadows of the strange night Robert could see the surcharge of mana leaping gold at the center of Scott's aura. Now. The moment had come, that fragment of time so long awaited, so often despaired of. Scott did not resist as Robert propelled him back to the wall of the parapet. "Look!" he commanded, "Look at the crest!"

Scott lifted his tormented face to the mountains, and Robert waited. There was no sound anywhere. At last, unable to bear it longer, he grasped Scott strongly by both shoulders.

"You speak of laws of honor . . . it's the stone gods, Manala!" he cried. "You once told me it was only the stone gods, Manala!"

Robert swayed, his mana ebbing. Manala looked with one brief, burning gaze into his eyes. "The Sun had nothing to do with it, Kapi," he said, and turned away to face the mountains.

Robert knew, as he made his way uncertainly out of the atrium, that Manala did not know he was alone. Robert saw that his gaze was fixed upon a holy crest.

M-level

Eve lay on her side, her eyes closed, drifting into sleep and then rousing, waiting for the next contraction. She was dimly aware that her baby would be born soon, but her weakness was so all-pervading that she could no longer care. Let it be as it will, she thought, with the baby and with me, too.

She was between sleep and non-sleep when, through the bars that guarded the side of her bed, she saw his hand, his immaculate ruffled cuff and the dark sleeve....

Unable to speak, she stretched both hands through the railing and clung to that hand, to that firm wrist. The pain came strongly and she felt him take both her hands in his. When it was over, she looked up and into his face. She could see him very clearly, and memory flooded, filling her.

"Beloved," he said, his face close to hers now, his beard brushing her cheek in the so-familiar way. "You are coming home, Beloved, back to the real."

"You have relented?" she whispered.

"No," he replied. "It is not that I have relented. It is rather that I have understood."

The drugs claimed her and she drowsed, but when she drifted closer to consciousness and roused, he was still holding her hand. She tried to comprehend, but her mind was vague. She was certain of nothing except a deep peace which seemed somehow to be familiar.

Someone was opening the curtains of her cubicle. "Let's see how you're doing, Mrs. Temple," said the nurse.

"I will come for you as always," promised Scott, and he was gone.

"Come now, Mrs. Temple," said the nurse. "Let's get your arms back inside the railing now, that's the girl."

IM-*level*

"I can divulge this much," said Higgins, "the Incomer has accepted the body of the child. The merger has already taken place."

Higgins, Max and Ida were now in the hospital corridor, waiting near the doors of the delivery room. At the end of the hallway they could see Warner, standing alone by the large window. Ida's heart reached out to him, but she withdrew her attention by an act of will, and faced Higgins.

"The merger has taken place? But Joel, what if something goes wrong—I mean, if the birth is too—if there is damage—what if the baby doesn't even make it?"

"Even so," replied Higgins, "he will pass through the birth trauma with her. It was his decision to do it this way."

"Joel—?"

Higgins was avoiding her eyes.

"Joel, who is it? Who's coming in?" she demanded.

"Please, Ida, I beg of you, don't put me in this position."

"You know who it is, Joel Higgins, you *know*. The picture is forming in your mind. I'm making it form. In spite of all that self-discipline of yours, you're seeing the

Incomer in your mind right now!" Her voice was growing shrill but Ida did not care.

Max was strangely silent. Ordinarily he would have tried to quiet her but now he stood lounging against the wall, watching her and Joel with an odd detachment. Okay, then, he was going to let her do what she could.

"I'm going to penetrate you, Joel," she said, grasping Higgins by both arms and fixing her eyes on his. "I'm going to penetrate you and I'm going to read you, Joel!"

Higgins attempted to avert his face but Ida pulled him back to meet her gaze, holding his face firmly between her hands.

"It's Bertram." Ida released him suddenly. "Joel, it's Bertram! You've known it all along!" She sagged against him and Higgins patted her shoulder awkwardly, his face crumpled.

Wiping her eyes with the back of her hand Ida looked carefully at Max. His green eyes met hers steadily, with a strange glint, but he did not speak.

"You, too. You knew it, too."

Both men were silent, watching her face.

"You could have told me," she said, feeling inexplicably on the defensive. "Listen, if I'd known he'd be with Eve and Warner ... that we could still communicate ... Don't you see? I could have stood it better."

Max came to her. "Darling," he said, his arm about her, wiping her tears with one finger in the familiar way, "you see? Do you see now? It's just a change. The form changes, honey, but the love stays. In all life, both sides, that's the way it is, the form changes. But we learn to keep on living, Ida. We keep on living."

"That's the trouble," she said with a trace of her old flippancy. "That's the whole damn trouble."

Down the corridor the doctor stood talking to Warner. Ida saw Warner's face, the relief and tenderness displayed so touchingly. Her throat ached again, looking at him.

"You want to know something? I wish I didn't love anybody," she cried passionately. "That's what louses up everything—the caring."

"I think we can go home now," said Max. "Come on. Let me louse up your life a little more."

Higgins was suddenly left alone to continue his vigil.

M-level

When at last the baby was brought to her, Eve had been sleeping deeply. For a moment it seemed to her that there was the scent of burning candles in the room and the sound of a fountain somewhere very near. In an instant the impression was gone, and Eve saw, with still bemused eyes, the small blanket-wrapped form as the nurse placed the tiny shape within her arms. The nurse was saying something, but Eve could not comprehend, and she was relieved when the nurse withdrew.

Eve unwrapped the blanket and looked for the first time upon him. A frail, too-thin baby, the dark smudges below his closed eyes had a faintly violet color. An infinitesimal vein pulsated near his temple. At the thought of the small heart laboring to sustain this fragile new life, Eve caught him to her, laying her warm cheek against his head, but in her weakness she could not support even so slight a burden, and turning upon her side she lay him, with great care, upon her pillow so that she could look into his sleeping face.

Half drowsing herself, Eve groped beneath his coverings and found a tight-curled fist. As if in response to her touch, the swollen eyelids opened and his eyes, the great blue, blind eyes of the newborn, seemed to gaze steadily into hers, unwavering, for an endless moment.

Eve's eyes blurred with tears.

"We'll make it," she whispered.

They slept.

Under Mary Kay's fingertips, the planchette glided smoothly over the panel of the new instrument. The conversation with Max was being automatically recorded, complete with punctuation marks. Unimpressed by the advance in interplane communication represented by this instrument, Mary Kay sat at the board, comfortable in jeans and bare feet. Kenneth, freed from his duties as recorder, lounged in his chair, observing intently.

"It'll be easier from now on, honey," spelled Max. "You don't have to be responsible any longer for the message between Scott and Eve. That's what I'm trying to tell you. Eve has remembered. Get it?"

"No, Max, I don't understand. Remembered what?"

"Her perception has opened up, wide up. The chakras, you know. She brings back memory of her night travel."

Mary Kay's fingers stopped the swaying planchette. She sat motionless, considering.

"What's the matter?" asked Kenneth, setting down his coffee cup. "Did it quit working?"

"What do you mean, has *it* quit working? I'm the one who stopped."

"What for?"

"Eve's chakras have opened up. I have to think about it."

"Her what have what?"

"Max," she said intently, ignoring Kenneth, "what about Warner? How can Eve—?"

Max had begun to spell again. "Don't worry, Mary, he said. "It's all right, doll."

"I don't see how. Her marriage—"

"Let's say the Planning Group people had their wits about them when they mapped out this contract."

"Then Eve won't need my work any more. Can I be free of it now? Just talk to you and Ida, like we used to do?"

"No, baby," answered Max, "you can't quit. We're going to be needing you. The baby has a tough trip ahead. We'll need a direct line available for him."

Max continued spelling. Mary Kay at last broke the motion of the planchette to dry her eyes. Kenneth got up from his chair and came over to her, bending over the instrument to read the typescript.

"It's becoming more and more obvious that we've tapped a creative level of your subconscious," he pronounced authoritatively, and then noticing her expression, "You have a terrifically creative sub," he added generously.

Mary Kay sighed, trying to remain hooked in to her psychic reverie.

"Max," she said at last, "it's that I'm never sure whether this communication is a good thing; I mean, maybe sometimes it would be better if the door stayed closed. I carry that concern all the time."

"I know you do," spelled Max. "I don't know, either,

whether it's good or bad, and I worry about it, too, just as you do. Maybe the truth is that it's some of each, like any form of communication. That's what Project Jupiter is all about, examining various facets of the matter. That's why so many experiments have had to be set up under the Project umbrella."

"You know," mused Kenneth, "it's not easy, tapping the subconscious area of the mind. Psychiatrists are still groping around with dream analysis—"

"Right," agreed Max, "and hypnosis and drugs and—"

"We may have uncovered another way," Kenneth continued. "Just to let the sub talk like this—"

"You mean like Ida and I talk on this writing machine?" asked Max.

"Oh, maybe not this one. My new model will have some improvements. But yes, that's the idea," Kenneth acknowledged. "Just to let the sub bring it all up and then let a shrink pick out what is useful, discarding the rest. Whatta you think?"

"Well, since you asked, I think that you are carrying on quite a conversation this very minute with a 'subconscious,' you realize that?"

"Why not?" retorted Kenneth. That's what the advantage is. Dream analysis, for instance, is a form of conversation, but our method might bypass the symbols used in dream language. Why, the possibilities—"

"Okay, pal," interrupted Max. "If Mary has Ida and me on call in her sub, how about putting YOURS on the line? Let's see who YOU'VE got tucked away down below? Whatcha say, ole buddy?"

Mary Kay glanced up at Kenneth. He looked the other way.

"Well, goodnight. Love and kisses," spelled Max, and was gone.

Mary Kay rose, rubbing the muscles of her lower back.

"*You* get the idea, don't you, hon?" persisted Kenneth.

Mary Kay eyed him levelly. "Sure," she said, "I get the idea."

It was a Friday, and Warner was glad to be able to get away from the office earlier than usual. Maybe he could hit the freeway ahead of the rush hour traffic. A half-hour, with luck, and then home, peace and rest. A blast of still, hot air struck him as he opened the door of his car. He shrugged out of his suit coat and loosened his tie. Indian summer, this oppressive, unseasonable heat, came very year, yet no one was ever prepared for it.

Ah, it would be great to have a dip in the pool before dinner. Too bad he'd covered it for the winter. If he'd known there would be only that one night of rain—but he had been restless while Eve had been in the hospital, had felt he should be getting things set for the wet winter months ahead.

When he reached home he saw, on the patio, the table covered with a brilliant orange cloth, the tall hurricane candles in place, a fire already laid in the fire ring. Warner felt a rush of pleasure and anticipation and he hurried into the kitchen.

Eve, looking tanned and fresh in a pink cotton pinafore, turned from the oven where she had been inspecting something in a pottery casserole that smelled deliciously of meat and wine.

"Oh, Warner, you're early!" she exclaimed, running across the cool brick floor and into his arms.

He was aware of her familiar light perfume and, mingled with it, the faint odor of baby spit-up from her slightly dampened shoulder. He felt a surge of contentment, followed by a deep tenderness.

"What kind of day did he have?" he asked, setting down his briefcase and draping his jacket over the back of a chair.

"Well, he kept down four ounces, last feeding," answered Eve, reaching for a wicker tray, "but he still has a lot of tummy pains. Do you want a drink, or is it too early?"

"Great!" he said. "God, it's hot today. I wish I hadn't covered the pool."

"Oh, it's just as well. It will rain again any day now."

"Where's Marsalina?" he asked, running water over an ice tray, "and the girls?"

"Kim had a nosebleed and Pam is being punished."

"What for?"

"For Kim's nosebleed," laughed Eve. "Marsalina is up there with them. I said Pam could get up when you came home and now here you are early."

"Let's keep it a secret," Warner grinned. "Can you sit down for a minute? Let's take these drinks out on the patio."

"In a second," she said. "Let me check the salad stuff first."

From the next room came the sudden thin wail of a baby in pain. Eve turned from the refrigerator, but Warner said quickly, "I'll get him."

Expertly, Warner covered his shoulder with the folded diaper which lay on the edge of the bassinette, and supporting the baby's head in his large hand he lifted the tiny, writhing body to his shoulder and began to pat.

"It's okay, son, okay now. I've got you . . ."

They lingered, lounging in the cushioned chairs beside the fire ring. The night had grown quickly cool as the breezes came down the canyon from the distant mountains. In the valley the lights of the city spread everywhere, wrapping around the dark hills like a jeweled sea. Eve studied Warner's face. In the glow of the fire it appeared touchingly dear and mortal. She felt her heart lurch with feeling.

"Warner," she said clearly, "I love you."

Warner turned his face to her, pleased.

"What brought that on, sweet? Did I do something special?"

"No, listen, I really love you, Warner Temple. Really and truly."

"Great!" replied Warner, adjusting the fire a bit. "And all this time I've thought you were in love with the TV repairman, the way he keeps showing up around here so often."

Eve did not answer.

"—or maybe the obstetrician, the way you keep coming back to him," he continued, smiling.

"Warner, stop kidding. I'm serious. I'm trying to tell you that I love you, that I'm so glad it's you—" and her voice broke slightly.

"Glad it's me?"

"Yes, I'm glad it's you ... for all the long years ahead. . . ." She could not go on.

Warner shifted uneasily in his chair. "You're over-tired, darling," he said with some concern, "up with the baby every night, and all. Let me get you a brandy. You deserve a good night's sleep."

"Warner, Warner, that's not it. I'm trying to tell you something."

"Look, Eve, I know you love me. I love you, too. So what's the trouble?"

"I want to be honest, utterly and completely honest with you, darling, because I love you too much to conceal anything from you."

"What terrible thing have you done? Ordered new carpeting or something?"

"No, nothing like that. It's—"

"—because that's okay, honey. I know the carpeting's beginning to—"

"Warner, do you believe love is universal? That there's no limit to it? That it's possible to love a child, a plant, a home, a city? And whole groups of people you don't even know, A father, a husband, a creative work? God? And it's all love? And no love diminishes or cancels out another love? There's love and love, and it's all love, all of it? Do you believe that, darling?"

"Evie, sweetheart, what's the matter? Are you flipping into a postpartum depression or something?"

"I'm not in any kind of depression, Warner. I'm happier than I've ever been in my life. And I can see things clearly now. I'm trying to tell you about it."

"So tell."

"Well, you know the psychic experiences I've had? Well, darling, I want to tell you, I want you to understand. You see, Warner, on the next plane—I know this is going to sound silly to you, but over there, see, darling, there's a man. A man—and I—this man and I—"

"Is that all?" smiled Warner. "You mean good old Max? I've figured all along that you and Mary Kay both had a crush on Max. That's what makes it fun for you girls. Sure, I understand."

"It's not Max, Warner, it's someone else. And it's not just a crush. I've had experiences—experiences I should tell you about."

Warner took her trembling hand in his big warm one. He spoke with calm assurance, "Eve, it's perfectly normal to have fantasies. Look, honey, I know all about these things, the psychological need some women have for the ideal, especially the unattainable ideal, and a spirit lover fills the bill. With a minimum cost. So if you are fantasizing about one of Max's spooks, don't feel guilty, honey, a little fantasizing is not going to hurt an emotionally stable girl like you, may even be good for you. Just as long as it's not some flesh-and-blood guy on *my* side of the street, I'm all for it. So if that's what's bothering you, you can quit worrying."

"But it's not fantasy. You call it that because you don't believe any of this spirit stuff. I have to explain it, Warner. It's a long story—"

"Too long a story for tonight, honey," he said good-naturedly, reaching for her other hand and pulling her up from her chair. "I've got to get up early and go in to the office for a little while in the morning, so let's get to bed." He extinguished the fire and came to her where she stood looking at him oddly. Hugging her affectionately, he said, "Looks like a nice weekend ahead, even with the pool covered."

Eve followed him silently as they entered the house. She helped him with the locking up and turning off of lights, securing their home for the night. Once, checking the pilot lights on the stove, she called to him, "Warner? All right, then," but he did not hear.

On the stairway going up to bed he put an arm about her waist companionably. "I knew there was something important for us to talk over tonight," he said. "I've got the life-insurance man coming in to see me tomorrow morning. I want to map out a good program for the baby's future."

Eve turned on the stair. "Good!" She smiled at him fondly. "That *is* important. He has a long haul ahead of him."

"Well, so do we, for that matter, another forty, fifty years, maybe, with luck."

"I know," she said slowly. "I told you, Warner, I'm so glad it's you."

During the night the baby slept fitfully. Eve attended to him quietly so as not to awaken Warner. At last, after his two o'clock feeding, he fell into a comfortable sleep. His cheeks were moist and tinged with healthy color, the upflung fists relaxed. He is better, thought Eve. I'm pulling him through.

There was still time for rest before the next feeding. Gratefully she went back to her bed, covering herself to the chin. The night is cold, she thought, and remembered her poem. "The night is cold, and I . . ." What was the rest of it? She could not recall. . . .

Drowsing, Eve heard the rain begin, the blessed rain . . . or was it a fountain, somewhere near? The light seemed faintly blue within the room, and on the air came the candle scent, the burning candles, unmistakable, thrilling . . .

She held her breath, and then, at last, it came ... that tiny sound, like the tearing of silk....

* * *

... for the Good will overcome the Evil; and the Light, Darkness; and the Life, Death. ... So be faithful, and live in that which doth not think the time long.
—GEORGE FOX

AFTERWORD

Addison dictated the closing words of this book to my sister Maurine and me on a summer evening in 1975 at my home in California. We were both swept by a variety of emotions, foremost among which, I think, was an enormous relief and sense of satisfaction that we had at last, after long effort and many difficulties, succeeded in recording his novel to his satisfaction. The end of Addison's book marked the end of a chapter, so to speak, in our experience with interplane communication.

Mediumship was not one of my youthful goals, nor was it Maurine's. Neither of us was aware of any psychic experiences dating back to childhood, which so many sensitives report. Our upbringing in a Quaker parsonage was not at all conducive to interest in the "occult," a subject viewed in our church environment as an aberration pursued by infidels, usually in California! The only conditioning I can see which may have had a bearing on our subsequent psychic work was that as Quakers we grew up with the reality of the Inner Light, and a respect for the Voice Within. Perhaps this practice of listening to the Voice prepared us for a later time when we would listen, mentally, for other impressions from a source not yet divine.

We began this adventure about thirty years ago, bringing to it the same skepticism and puzzlement as any other novices would certainly feel. Our automatic writing produced no earth-shaking revelations, no verifiable predictions, no scientific evidence of survival after death. We simply carried on conversations with a group of people claiming to be spirits, in the course of which over a period of several years their personalities emerged with such vividness and such consistency that we eventually gave up our amateurish efforts to establish "evidence" which would prove whether or not these new friends were what they purported to be, and gave ourselves over to receiving whatever they had to say. We were drawn by a gradual and natural process in which we met them at the border between their world and ours and merged with them in consciousness from time to time, much as the ocean tide moving in upon the shore, and out again, takes with it the tiny sands of the beach.

From the very beginning we failed to receive the kind of messages we were expecting from the "Beyond," such cliff-hangers, for instance, as "I am happy here" or "Do not grieve." Far from delivering to us this kind of bland reassurance, our friends on the IM-level seemed to have retained the human proclivity for self-interest. Along with the "spiritual teachings" which we extracted from them (and which of course made us feel a lot better about the whole thing!), we received accounts from these friends concerning their present condition. A composer shared with us the outline of the opera he was working on, entitled "Iscariot," in which he was presenting a startling and, to us, a revolutionary characterization of Judas. Our chief communicator, Abe Kaufman, thinly disguised in this book as Max Melchior, and Ida, not at all disguised, expressed vividly the involvements and problems of their lives. Ida was becoming intrigued with and challenged by psychotherapy as practiced on the IM-level. Abe was struggling with an on-going problem with the staff of his treatment center. Another friend had found love and fulfillment. One dear friend complained that she could not adjust to so much emphasis on creating one's desires mentally. She yearned to get her hands into "a pan of good hot soapy dishwater—*real* water!"

Our communicators suffered the pain of bereavement, the stresses of accommodating to change, and the difficulties of personal relationships. They had moods. They faced disappointments and endured frustrations. But they also experienced pleasure and joy and happiness—to about the same degree and in much the same way that we were experiencing it on our level. They learned; they modified ideas; they matured as time passed. In short, these people were really *living*, it seemed to us. As Addison says of Max, they had been transformed into neither saints nor demons by their transition to the IM-level. They were continuing to cope with life with whatever equipment their backgrounds and states of development provided.

One of these friends was known to us simply as "Addison." He was a writer both by inclination and by profession throughout his mortal lifetime, which was during the nineteenth century in New England. His manner of expression still retained the elegance and the formality of the educated man of his period. We were intrigued, entertained, and sometimes amused when we received his comments on some present-time occurrence, couched in his elaborate Victorian speech. Addison had been a member of a group of intellectuals, among them several writers, who advanced concepts which were ahead of their time in terms of Western thought. He lived out his mortal years in accordance with those principles. He told us recently, however, while we were working with him on this book, that in retrospect he is no longer impressed by the ideas which had so electrified that group. Other concerns now seem to him to be more relevant to the progress of the soul. We knew that he was continuing to write on the IM-level, but our desire to receive samples of his present-day style was frustrated by the crudity of our simple Ouija board as a communication tool. Addison, too, was exasperated by what he called our "mutilation" of his work as we attempted to receive it, and he always gave it up.

The shortcomings of the Ouija board as a means of recording psychic pick-ups with any degree of precision are perfectly obvious to anyone who has tried it. The simple alphabet, without provision for punctuation or spacing, leaves opportunity for error. In our experience we have sometimes had difficulty in agreeing on the exact wording or spelling of even a single sentence. We have cut off the entity in mid-sentence, assuming that the thought had been satisfactorily expressed. We have interpreted as a statement what was intended as a question. Thus the margin for confusion and inaccurate understanding is considerable, and may well account, in part, for the low regard in which the Ouija board is held by psychical researchers.

We communicated in this slow and tedious way for many years. We were hampered, also, by the fact that Maurine lived on the east coast with her family and I with mine on the west, so that we had to make the most of such opportunities as arose for us to get together. Further, my husband regarded my psychic pursuits as an absurdity on my part which he would tolerate in silence—a silence expressive enough so that I tended to feel most like operating the board while he was safely away at work! Later, he came to value our work and has been supportive in every possible way.

Maurine's husband, Kenneth Wilcoxon, worked in naval research programs throughout his career. His background in science made it natural that his approach to our psychic work would differ from my husband's, and from Maurine's and mine, as well. Kenneth was not greatly interested in our discussions with our spirit friends concerning such things as philosophy, spiritual laws that govern "progress," and their descriptions of life as they were individually experiencing it on their level. He did not have a preference as to whether we were tapping our own subconscious reservoirs or whether we were indeed in telepathic contact with people who had died. To him, one explanation seemed just as reasonable as the other. He *did* feel that we were producing material without our own conscious effort, and he wanted to pursue the work under improved conditions.

When Ken retired from naval research, he was able

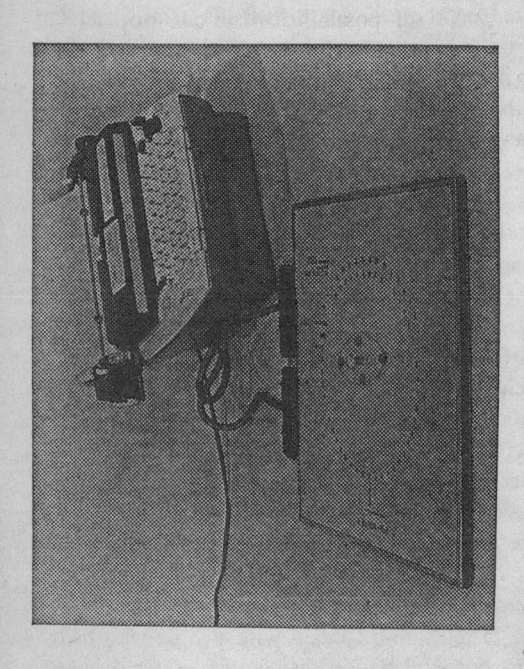

The Psi-Writer. The board is 16 inches by 16 inches and ½-inch thick, covered with a transparent acrylic sheet for easy planchette movement and durability. The planchette is of transparent, rigid plexiglass with the permanent magnet fixed in its center. Made by Wilcoxon Research, 12526 Parklawn Drive, Rockville, Md. 20852.

to devote more time to his electronics firm, which also specialized in research, and to the needs of our psychic work. Aware of the necessity for overcoming the limitations of the Ouija board and wanting to provide an accurate record of the conversations, free from any interpolations on our part, Kenneth developed and produced the Wilcoxon Psi-Writer. This new instrument opened up a world of possibilities for our work. The spelling board of the Psi-Writer is laid out in a circular arrangement which includes the alphabet, punctuation marks, space and carriage return. The board is electrically connected to a typewriter. A magnet is located in the center of the planchette, and as it moves over a character, the magnet closes a switch and causes the electric typewriter to type that character. Thus, the communicating entity is able to spell, space and punctuate exactly as he or she wishes, with a permanent record being printed as the communication comes through.

Maurine and Kenneth brought the first model of the Psi-Writer from Washington, D.C. to my home in California in 1971. Shortly after our work session began, our long-accustomed practice of using our board for personal conversations was interrupted. Addison, instead of his customary greetings, began to spell out: "It was dark at first when she entered the room and she did not know he was standing at the entrance to the atrium." Maurine and I literally held our breath as the planchette moved steadily until we had recorded the brief scene in its entirety. Addison was using his allotment of time and vital force to give us, at last, an excerpt from his work. Fascinated, we asked him to tell us more about it. He said he had read to us a fragment from his new novel.

The Psi-Writer had so improved the ease and accuracy of communication that all of us could see the possiblity of undertaking the transcription of his entire book. Addison was pleased at the prospect of sharing his work with us; however, he explained that he had composed the novel for a readership on the IM-level and that it was replete with situations, references and terminology which would be incomprehensible to mortal readers. It would require a complete rewrite, he said, to give the story any reality for readers on our mortal level. He set about at once to do the rewrite, and gave the book the working title of "The M-Translation." Much later he said that he would prefer some other title for publication, and suggested several. "The Jupiter Experiment" was agreed upon by all concerned.

Our mortal team was now launched upon a project which has so far covered a period of four years, during which our task has been to manage semi-annual trips of several weeks each between California and Washington, in order to record, up to this writing, a total of four books. Of these four, *Wedge* and *The Jupiter Experiment* are now published; the remaining ones will follow. One of the books is a continuation of the story of Wedge; the other, which we hope to finish in 1976, is drawn from Ida's case-history material. The IM-team has had the responsibility of producing the material and of deciding which spirit was going to dictate a book next.

We were well into the recording of "The M-Translation" when Wedge made his appearance, and we had to lay aside the Translation in order to accommodate his needs, and to receive from him, over a period of two years, his recalls of his mortal life. Readers of this book, entitled simply *Wedge* (Llewellyn Publications, 1975), will understand why our involvement with Wedge necessitated our interrupting Addison's dictation. For a while we attempted to work on both books during a single session, receiving from Wedge in the morning hours, setting aside the afternoon for Addison, and reserving the evening for our personal work with Wedge. Of course it did not work out. The mechanics of our mediumship involve a complicated telepathic procedure in which Maurine and I "pick up" a letter, word or group of words from the communicating entity which we register in some area of our minds below consciousness, and involuntarily move the planchette, causing it to spell. We were able to receive smoothly enough during the first board session of the day, but when we attempted to leave Wedge's book and turn our attention to Addison's, we so frequently distorted the passages we were trying to receive that at one point Addison said, in frustration, that his enthusiasm for publication was rapidly evaporating. Finally he said that he would prefer to wait until we had finished with Wedge's dictation and were able to focus properly on "The Jupiter Experiment," as it is now called.

Working with Addison was an entirely different experience from receiving *Wedge*. Wedge's book was published exactly as we received it, including spelling—a rustic form of Elizabethan English. Addison, like most writers, I suppose, rearranged the sequence of scenes, rewrote lines, deleted whole segments, some of which were our favorites, and added new scenes. Occasionally he would ask us to suggest a word or phrase, particularly when he was writing present-time conversation. Always we worked with a sense of fleeting time, the deadline coming ever closer when we must end the session and return to our homes. For this reason, we were unable to ask Addison the countless questions which we would have so much liked to have him answer, questions about the concepts he was expressing.

Some of these we had known about throughout the years of our conversations with the IM-level. For example, we were familiar with the idea of out-of-body travel; we knew that the immortals we were contacting were dwellers on the very next level of consciousness, having but recently given up "the burdens and the blessings" of mortal life; that they called their level the astral plane; that there are other higher levels to which one progresses in steps; that some of these immortals believed in reincarnation and that others did not. We had been told a little about the Jupiter Experiment, an experiment designed on the IM-level, the purpose of which was to observe and record efforts on both levels to communicate, and to record and evaluate the results of any successful communication, as well as the results of garbled communication. We knew that under the umbrella label of Jupiter, many individual projects were being set up and carried out, that ours was only a part of a vast network. The scope of the Experiment was so vast, we were told, that our friends on the IM could only vaguely comprehend it.

We were, on the other hand, not familiar with the Planning Group, nor the exact nature of "contracts" or "commitments." We would like to ask Addison whether there is a difference between the "aura" and the "auric field." What exactly is a "communicator"? In order to "penetrate," or "conduct a probe," how does one go about it? How, oh how, does one "recharge"? Do mortals have these capacities too, if only they knew how to put them to use? We are able, at this point, to grasp only vaguely what these terms mean.

Above all, I wonder how literally we are to take *The Jupiter Experiment*. We know that Addison rewrote the original version in order to make it meaningful to us, limited as we are to our mortal frame of reference. Therefore, he has expressed his concepts through the experiences of his characters—experiences with which mortals can identify. Which of them are literal? Well, as this book goes to press, we do not know. How literal are the biblical streets of gold and walls of jasper? The bridge, the river, Scott's mountains—for that matter, Harriet's hamburger, Ida's champagne, Max's steaming mug of coffee. Literally true? For my part, I rather hope they are very literal indeed. At any rate, from Addison's story it seems to me that an overall picture emerges of life immediately following death—at least, insofar as this particular group of individuals are experiencing it—a manner of existence with which I feel I could cope and in which I could continue to grow. I doubt that Addison intended this book to be a delineation of immortal life, in general, any more than Mark Twain's or Sinclair Lewis' or John Steinbeck's books lay claim to being totally representative of life on the mortal level.

The reader will, of course, read this book according to his own Inner Light—that "true light which lighteth every man" and woman (John 1:9). We are passing on to the reader Addison's story, which we feel will entertain, at the very least, and at the most, offer food for thought.

—MARGARET MOON
COLTON, CALIFORNIA, 1976

for further reading in the psychic realm
WEDGE, Llewellyn Publications, Box 3383, St. Paul, MN 55165, $3.95

Margaret and Maurine Moon were deeply into the recording of *The M-Translation* (the working title of *The Jupiter Experiment*) via the Psi-writer when transmissions from another spirit began to interfere. They attempted to deal with both communicators, but it soon became apparent that all of the sisters' attention would have to be devoted to the urgent messages which came to be known, in book form, as *Wedge*.

Wedge is the autobiography of a 17th-century spirit, Jude Wedge. It describes his life and early death as a boy in England, and his experiences as a companion spirit to his older brother as they voyage to and settle in the "New Land" of America. In a collage of brief, engaging vignettes narrated in a quaint rustic idiom, *Wedge* reveals much about early colonial America.

More than a historical novel, it reveals also the special problems and needs of a soul too soon deprived of physical life. It features an aspect of spiritual reality rarely treated with sympthy and without fear—the earthbound spirit's being helped from this side instead of being cast out like a demon.

Wedge is the result of a unique, unorthodox form of therapy which involves the interaction of those on both mortal and immortal levels in getting the earthbound spirit to accept his death and immortality. The story of this therapy, told in the Introduction and Epilogue, is humorous, touching—and profound, for those who read Wedge's story on its deepest level.